BLACK MADONNA

The Pope's Obsession

L Lee Kane

TSL Publications

First published in Great Britain in 2019
By TSL Publications, Rickmansworth

Copyright © 2019 L Lee Kane

ISBN / 978-1-913294-10-6

Dedication

For Robin C Kane
And a long life together

Fantastic Mystery/History Thriller Like No Other

A MUST READ!

May 1, 2019

I received a free copy of this book in exchange for a fair and honest review. All opinions are my own.

A lifetime of tragedy leads a young woman into a centuries-old battle between two ancient orders over a secret that could change the world forever in author Linda Lee Kane's *Black Madonna: A Pope's Deadly Obsession*.

Review

This was a fast paced, action packed history thriller like no other. The mystery of the novel comes in two parts: the first being the mystery behind the secret the church has been chasing all these centuries, and the second being who was being the deaths of Luci's parents and others in her life. The story thrives when it delves into the mythology aspect of the narrative, which readers will find refreshing as it flips the book on specific aspects of religion and history when it comes to the Catholic Church.

Exploring aspects like how Tarot Cards were marked as "evil" by the church, the secret teachings of Jesus of Nazareth (whether you believe in him as the Lord or are interested from a historical stand-point, this book will fascinate you regardless), and the lengths an organization will go to in order to maintain power and control, this novel features a truly amazing narrative. While there are some great character developments in this novel, it is the mystery and mythology of the book that really shines through, showcasing a powerful command over history and religion's impact on humanity overall on the author's part.

Verdict

This is a must read novel for any historical fiction and mystery fans out there. Filled with action, suspense and a twisting plot that will leave readers on the edge of their seat, this is a unique read that readers rarely glimpse in the historical fiction genre. If you haven't yet, be sure to grab your copy of *Black Madonna: The Pope's Obsession* by Linda Lee Kane today!

How the History of the Cathars was hidden in the Tarot of Marseilles

For some time I have believed there is a connection between a religious group called the Cathars who became a dominant influence during the twelfth and thirteenth centuries and the historical figures of that period and images in the tarot cards. In addition to retelling the story of the Cathar era, the personal messages of the Cathars also found a place in the tarot cards. In his book, *The Tarot*, Alfred Douglas writes, "It has been suggested that the tarot cards might have been produced by Cathars as a means of representing their stories pictorially to those who were illiterate." I've picked up several tarot decks of cards so I could better understand them and how they translate pictorially but it was interesting to take this theory of the pivotal characters of the Albigensian War and some of the spiritual messages of the Cathars to reveal how this page of history became secretly concealed with the Tarot of Marseilles. Here is some of the information I've gleaned from the interpretations,

The Magician card: Simon Magus, or Simon the Magician was called the Father of Heresy. He was given this title after being accused of attempting to purchase the power of the Holy Spirit from the apostles for his own personal gain. From this we get the term "simony", the sin of buying spiritual favor from Simon Magus. Another name was also used in the tarot for The Magician. It was Le Jongleur, or The Juggler. No one knows why, but in 1195 at the age of forty-five Folques gave up his life as a troubadour and joined the Cistercian Order of monks. From there he rose to prominence and became a Bishop. Bishop Folques was disliked by the people of Toulouse and they called him the "bishop of devils". He was also described as the anti-Christ. And it may have been the intention of the creators of the Tarot of Marseilles to use the Jongleur to cleverly disguise Bishop Foulques in the first card.

The Popess: Historically, there is no real evidence of there ever being a female pope. Therefore, it is interesting that this card is included in the tarot. There was a legend of a woman pope named Joan who became popular from the thirteenth century. She is said to have been pope around 1099, during a time when there were several "antipopes". From the earliest appearance of the card, the Popess has indicated a heretical theme and implies a challenge to the Catholic faith. In one citation Moakley tells us that the Popess may have a reference to Manfreda Visconti, a first cousin of Matteo Visconti, who became a patron of the early Italian tarot decks. Manfreda served as the abbess of the Umiliati Order of Nuns, and was declared Pope of Milan in 1300. In the tarot cards she is pictured wearing a nun's brown habit as opposed to a pope's gown. She also wears a three-tiered tiara. We might assume she is being portrayed with the same level of authority as the Roman Catholic Pope. The Popess may represent the Cathars in this earthly realm and is shown with an open book on her lap, unlike her depiction in the Bisconti tarot where the book is closed.

The Empress: In the tarot, the Empress represents the ultimate expression of the medieval woman, both temporally and spiritually. The images of the women on the cards are significant as shown by the inclusion of the Poppess, the Empress, Temperance, Justice and Force. It is also important to remember the Queen to the four suits because of the impact women had during the Albigensian Crusade. Another interesting suggestion is that of The Virgin Mary as the true Empress of the world. The Empress with the Virgin Mary can also be found in the language of the literature of the times. The expression "Virgin Empress" appears in *The Song of the Cathar Wars*, written by witnesses of the Albigensian Crusade. In the verse the author writes: "But by Saint Mary Virgin Empress, I would rather die by the sword and shining steel than let them keep us crushed and helpless." Although there is a reason to believe that the Empress may have been associated with the Virgin Mary and the patronesses of Languedoc, we cannot dismiss the possibility of the card's reference to Blanche of Castile, who married King Louis VIII and became Queen of France in 1223.

The Emperor: The pillars that hold up the world are represented by the pope, the other the Emperor. The spiritual world was ruled by the pope and the political world belonged to the Emperor. Sometimes these two worlds blurred, mainly when it involved money and land. In 1300 everything came crashing down when Pope Boniface VIII changed the pope's crown to the triple tiara, indicating his status about the king and emperor. The tarot shows the Emperor not standing forward but as a profile with his back to the pope showing defiance or possibly that Raymond VI showed one face to the pope but secretly showed sympathy to the Cathars.

The Pope: In the fifth card of the major arcana Cathars who willingly chose death rather than renounce their faith.

The Hermit: The twelfth century was witness to many dissenting preachers. Wandering from town to town, the holy men lived the lives of a hermit, challenging orthodox religious ideas which often labelled them as heretics. Peter of Bruys, a critic of the church was often found preaching in Toulouse. He had once been a priest but lost his station when he began burning crosses, declaring them empty icons.

The Wheel of Fortune: According to the Cathars, man goes through a series of transmigrations on earth before reaching the Last Judgement. In the Tarot of Marseilles decks, the figure at the top of the wheel wears a crown. However, this position is temporary, as all things change. The lesson is that spiritual man is required to choose goodness, and in this way, he prevents himself from being drawn downward into the realm of a base animal.

Force: Represents the virtue of Fortitude, definitely something demanded of the southern forces in a time of war. The Lion represents the enemies of the Albigensian. It may refer to King Louis VIII of France, who was called The Lion. It was the Lion who launched the crusade against the Albigensians and brought down Count Raymond VII.

The Hanged Man: I begin the prologue with a man being hung upside down and the card has sometimes been called The Traitor probably taken from the "shame paintings of the time". A famous character in the Albigensian war is Count Raymond VI's own brother, Baldwin, who switched loyalties to fight on the side of the crusaders. When Baldwin was captured, Raymond had him hanged as a traitor, describing him as "far worse than Cain".

Temperance: Normally the card is represented by a woman pouring water from one jar to another but in the Tarot of Marseilles, she is shown as an angel. She is conspicuously placed between Death and the Devil.

The Devil: It speaks of the dual nature of man, shown in the card with a man and woman in shackles, bound by the devil. The antlers which the man and woman in the card are wearing add to this theme. If you are looking for a specific person of the time who might represent the Devil it would have to be Jacques Fornier, the most feared and infamous Inquisitor of his time. He was responsible for hundreds of arrests, trials, and punishments of accused heretics. In 1334 he was elected pope at Avignon and took the name Benedict XII. He kept copious notes of trials he held and was known as "a devil of an Inquisitor".

The Tower: Possibly meant to represent a military structure. The most legendary outposts of the Cathars was Montsegur, in the country of Foix. The fall of Montsegur is accepted as the Cathars' final military defeat.

The Star: In this card we are shifting into a more spiritual phase and our focus is on the divine through the astrological bodies of the Star, the Moon, and the Sun. The star often represents the guiding light that led the magi to Jesus. The symbol of the pregnant woman on the Star may also be associated with the monastic tradition of helping those in need. The Star card comes after the Tower – after the fall of Montsegur. The Cathar elite have been killed and the counts of Toulouse defeated, but there is hope that their souls and teachings will survive.

The Moon: After the Star is the Moon card eclipsing the sun. For my story it could represent the difficult situation the Cathars found themselves in at the time, where secrecy and disguise became their only method of survival.

The Sun: Instead of just a Sun as once depicted on earlier tarot cards, this one has two youths who take center stage. These two children could represent Jeanne, the only daughter of Count Raymond VII, and her young husband Alphonse. At the age of nine they were promised in marriage upon the Treaty of Paris of 1229. The treaty was signed on Holy Thursday, 12 April – the beginning of the Easter Celebration of Christ's death and resurrection. The card depicts the end of the house of the counts of Toulouse, but also a period of growth and renewal after twenty years of warfare. The children are shown inside a common wall, suggesting the union of the house of St Gilles and the French king.

Judgment: For medieval man, the Last Judgement was a very real event. One of the basic heresies of Christianity involves the debate as to whether Jesus was a man, God, or a combination of both. The Cathars believed that Christ could not have been human, since the material body is evil. Therefore if Christ was not of this world, then the Crucifixion and Resurrection were false. They believed that the Resurrection was not to be taken literally, but rather as a spiritual awakening.

The World: the last card we see is of a person who has become enlightened and is surrounded by Mathew, Luke, Mark, and John. In the Tarot of Marseilles it represents the gospels and their importance. The wreath may also have significance because a wreath at that time represented triumph.

The Fool. We have come full circle. We have come through the trials and tribulations of the Magician through the events of the Albigensian Wars. You will meet the men and women of this time, the Count of Touslouse Simon de Montfort, Pope Innocent III, Bishop Fulks (Folques), the heretic monks and the Cathar Prefects.

Prologue

The Hanged Man

*Anyone who attempts to construe a personal view of God which conflicts
with Church dogma must be burned without pity.*
~ Pope Innocent III

Toulouse, France, 1209
Guilhelm de Montanhagol, a Knights Templar, knew his death
was imminent. Few who entered the halls of torment emerged
whole in mind or body. For six years, Bishop Folques had kept
him imprisoned in a small cell in Toulouse. Condemned as a
heretic, he'd suffered the agony of the rack on several occasions.

He reflected on the last time Folques visited him in the dungeon.
He had been splayed on a board, tied down at the wrists and
ankles. Rollers at each end of the board slowly turned, pulling his
body in opposite directions until every joint dislocated. He could
no longer sit or stand. He slept, ate, and wasted away in his own
filth. His once fine kirtle and linen shirt were just rags wrapped
around his body for warmth.

His thoughts turned to his lover, Esclarmonde. Thinking of her
comforted him in his last hours. Esclarmonde's skin was the color
of alabaster, her shimmering blonde hair, highlighted with wisps
of silver, cascaded down her body. She favored floor-length, loose-
ly fitted gowns, usually of blue. He longed to thread his hands
through her hair one last time. Her emerald-green eyes shimmered
with love for him. Esclarmonde was strong. She would get the
codex, written by Mary Magdalene, safely away.

Guilhelm was at peace in this knowledge. He was ready to accept
his impending death. His tormentors had beaten him down men-
tally and physically. Esclarmonde was gone. His brothers in the

Knights Templar were dead and gone. There was no hope, only the desire to die and end the suffering.

Soldiers came, stripped him of the last of his ragged clothing, then dragged him from his meager cell. He had been wearing the same clothes he had worn since Pope Innocent III had him thrown into this God-forsaken hell. They hung him upside down by one leg, creating the sensation of a crucifixion. In time, this posture would inhibit and exhaust the muscles required for breathing. They stretched him in one direction, while gravity and his body weight worked against him. Exhaustion would eventually set in, and he would die. They do this to traitors, he thought angrily, but he was not a traitor. He was a Knights Templar and had sworn an oath never to kill a Christian. The pope believed if one was not of the Orthodox Christian faith, then the person was a heretic and should pay for his crimes against the church. Today, Folques, dressed in monk's attire, came to offer Guilhelm a last salvation if he would only give up his lover's secret, the treasure hidden by the Cathars, people who practised a religion the pope had declared war against in 1208.

"You must be getting desperate, Folques," Guilhelm whispered weakly. "I have not seen you in years. Have the Cathars escaped with the secret you want so desperately so you can protect the pope and the Roman religion?"

"Guilhelm, tell me where the treasure is hidden, and I will spare you from being tortured further," Folques coaxed, while nervously shuffling a deck of cards in his hands.

"I believe the end is near, Bishop. I have nothing to gain and everything to lose in telling you anything. I would lose my soul if you were to extort that from me," Guilhelm proclaimed defiantly.

Folques held out a card for Guilhelm who strained through blurred vision to see its face. He saw what appeared to be a young woman holding open the jaws of a lion. He's discovered cards, he thought. He blinked back the salty sweat rolling down his face, trying to see more clearly.

The image faded and he saw a Roman pontiff holding a staff, crowned by the Yellow Cross of the Cathars. The next card Folques pulled from the deck displayed a burning tower with its defenders leaping to their deaths. Visions of the cards floated past Guilhelm with greater speed, a blur of scenes he could barely distinguish through his battered eyes. Did this mean that Esclarmonde's plan had worked? His mind leaped with joy as his body grew weaker. God bless Esclarmonde.

"Who is this woman?" Folques demanded again.

The question roused Guilhelm from his anguished thoughts. The guards yanked his head back by his hair. He saw Foulques displaying a card with a hand-painted miniature of his beloved Esclarmonde.

"We found these playing cards being copied and passed from city to city like holy relics by gypsies. What is their purpose?" Folques demanded.

Guilhelm suddenly turned away, realizing which card Folques was holding – the one that depicted the seated priestess. She held a scroll bearing the letter's tarot. Esclarmonde created these cards to preserve the teachings of the Cathars for future generations. The scroll protected by the High Priestess would one day turn the world upside-down, but only if the truth was known.

Two burly guards cut Guilhelm down and let him drop hard to the ground. Grabbing him by his arms, they picked him up and gripped his head, turning it to face the pyre. He felt the intense heat and smelled the smoke. He envisioned Esclarmonde calling out to him.

He had withstood more pain than most men could have. Completely worn out, he longed only to be with his lover one day in the Hereafter.

"Tell me, Guilhelm, now," ordered Folques.

Guilhelm forced a slight smile on his dry, cracked lips, knowing that one day the truth about the Cathars and the treasure would be known.

"Your god is waiting for you and every other Cathar," Folques spat out with disgust. "I will find the treasure of the Cathars if it takes killing every one of you." He turned to the guards. "He might as well burn. He is useless to me."

The Wheel of Fortune

The time will come when every change will cease,
This quick revolving wheel shall rest in peace.
~ Francesco Petrarch, I Trionfi

Present Day
"Luci, you little fish, get out of the pool. We have a dinner engagement with your daddy's clients in Big Sur and it's going to take us about an hour to get there, so hurry up."

"Okay, Mom, but the water feels so good after my karate lesson."

"I'm sure it does but you need to hustle. We have dinner reservations and we don't want to be late."

"Can I wear the new dress that Uncle Nicholas sent me from France?"

"Don't you think that's a little too sophisticated for a girl who's only eight years old?"

Mom always answered a question with a question. She wanted to make Luci think about what she was saying so she could make the right decision – hers. "Not if we lived in France. And, anyway, I will be nine in four more months," Luci jumped off the red and blue raft and swam to the side of the pool.

"You're such a precocious child, but if you hurry up, I'll let you wear it."

Luci gazed up at her mom as she wrapped a striped red and white towel, warmed by the sun, around her shoulders. Her mom had eyes the color of an arctic storm, similar to a photograph she had seen by a local artist: light ice blue with shades of deep blue. Luci had seen the photographer and his artwork at a fair in Ventura a few weeks back. His photographs of the Arctic and the polar bears thrilled her, and the soft colors reminded her of her mom.

Luci quickly dried off, raced to the back door of the garage, then ran into the laundry room, throwing her towel on top of the washing machine. She headed directly to her room.

Combing her tangled wet hair out, she tied it back into a pony-tail, then pulled the beautiful golden dress that smelled as if it had been sprinkled with cinnamon from the closet and slipped it on.

Luci grabbed the doorknob, opened her bedroom door, ran into the hallway, and stopped when she saw her father and heard him speaking angrily on the phone.

"The diary you are seeking, Father, is not for sale. You have called repeatedly and I have given you my answer. As long as I am alive, that diary will be protected from people like you," he said with a glint of fire in his gray eyes. He hung up the phone quickly.

Looking around, Dad spotted Luci just coming out of her room. "Come on, we're waiting for you," he said impatiently.

"Coming, Dad," she responded.

She had never heard her father raise his voice. He was a college professor who spoke softly to everyone, but with authority. The only bad thing anyone ever said about her father was that he had incredibly bad taste in bow ties, and she would have to agree.

Turning toward Luci, her dad perked up. "Wow, you look like a princess in your new dress, sugar pops."

"Dad, stop calling me that," she giggled. "I'm almost nine and none of my friends have nicknames like that."

Her mom walked into the living room where Luci and her dad were talking, carrying Luci's stuffed bear. "Here's Teddy, Luci. He keeps a secret safe within him so always keep him close," her mom, reminded her.

On her eighth birthday, Luci's mom had given her the teddy. All of the kids in the neighborhood had this animal and Luci had begged for one. They came in blue, purple, and pink and all had a heart inside. She had watched from behind her mom's bedroom door as her mom pulled out the heart and tucked an old key inside the heart. Luci never let on that she knew what was hiding inside it.

Taking hold of her stuffed animal, Luci jumped into the backseat of her dad's shiny new car. She loved its blue color and the white leather seats. She inhaled deeply, soaking in the scent of the new car.

Smiling, her dad put the car into gear and off they headed to a French restaurant that overlooked the Pacific Ocean.

Her parents were laughing and singing a song written by Bo Diddley. *They are so out of date*, Luci thought. What she wouldn't give to be listening to Taylor Swift.

As they drove along the cliff's edge, Luci peered out the window and saw green trees and the sprouting of orange California Poppies sprinkled along the mountainside by the water.

"Hey, sugar pops, take a look at the beautiful ocean and the silent golden dish falling behind the horizon," her dad said with a grin.

Luci closed her eyes and felt the warmth of the sun penetrating her eyelids. The sun always followed her. Sometimes she felt magical, like she could control the sun and do anything while in its spotlight.

But she was growing up and her childhood dreams had to be pushed aside. "Oh, Dad, really?" she answered. "I'm taking geography, and Christopher Columbus would never have sailed the 'ocean blue' if he thought he was going to fall off."

Her dad wasn't listening. She could see panic in his eyes as he glanced back in the rear-view mirror.

"Monica, I can't slow down. The breaks aren't working."

Luci watched from the back seat as her dad gripped the wheel. His knuckles were turning white and his face lost its color.

He pumped the brakes repeatedly, but the car wasn't slowing down. A sharp turn around the edge of the mountainside was up ahead.

"Yank back on the gear shift!" her mom screamed as a big rig came around the bend ahead of them.

"*I can't. I tried.* The car is speeding up, and I'm losing control!" her father yelled.

Ice-cold fear ran through her as she heard her mother's screams. Her father reached around to the back seat and pushed Luci down to the floor. Suddenly, their brand-new car slammed into the back end of a truck and traveled, as if in slow motion, down an embankment. Luci could hear glass breaking as tree limbs sliced through the windows. The car bounced and twisted down the mountain, jolting Luci around as she crouched close to the floor, holding on to Teddy. And then, one loud *bang* as the car slammed into something solid. The sound echoed against the mountain, forcing Luci to cover her ears.

An eerie silence followed, as if every sound had been swallowed up completely. Luci could only hear the crashing of the waves against the cliff. Her head was stretched backward and all she could see were the tops of the trees as they loomed overhead. The dark shimmering leaves blotted out the night sky but for one patch where the moon shone through. Smoke began to fill the car. She couldn't see or hear her parents. The smoke was overwhelming and she couldn't breathe. Wedged between the back and front seats, she was pinned down in the mangled car. Luci cried out for her mom and dad, but only heard her own voice echo back to her. Then she began screaming wildly as terror took hold. She couldn't stop screaming. She wanted her parents to hear her, to answer her calls, but there was no response, and her world collapsed.

She pushed against the seat and tried to claw her way up from the floor of the car. She could hear the wail of the fire engines coming closer. Someone was screaming and crying. It was her own voice, she realized, and it terrified her.

Luci couldn't see through the stinging smoke, but her hearing became more acute. She heard footsteps sliding down the loose dirt.

"Is anyone there?" the man said in a deep voice. Could it be the truck driver coming back? Soon, there were more footsteps. She heard the loud whoosh of a forceful spray of water against the car.

"Hello? Can anyone hear me?" the man asked. "Is there anyone in the car?"

Luci was whimpering. She couldn't get any air into her lungs. When she took a breath, she coughed and gasped from the heavy smoke that sought to keep her down. Just then, a burly firefighter reached through the back window, ripped out the seat cushion that was trapping her, and gently lifted her out of the car.

"I need my mom and dad. Where are they?" she cried.

"Hush, sweetheart. We'll take everyone to the hospital. Look, I found a teddy bear. Is it yours?" the firefighter asked.

Hitting him with all her strength, she yelled, "I want my mom and dad! Where are they?" She screamed through a flood of tears.

The firefighter handed her the teddy bear, then, slipping on the loose dirt while holding Luci tightly he climbed back up the hill.

Luci held Teddy against her chest. The firefighter turned to glance behind him at a paramedic. "The Olds just missed flying over that cliff."

Luci snuggled her head up against the firefighter's, finding comfort in the rhythm of his heart. At the ridge top, he gently placed her in the care of the paramedic, who quickly whisked her away in the ambulance to the Monterey Peninsula Community Hospital.

† † †

The sun was just coming up over El Bosque Drive early the next morning. Rays of sunshine beamed through a window. Luci looked down to see her leg covered in a cast. Groggy, she glanced around the room. Stark reality hit her as she surveyed the cold, pale walls. She moaned in pain. A nurse appeared around the doorway and ran to her side. She cradled her in her arms, feeling the heaving and rolling of her chest as her cries became spasms and then lapsed into soft whimpers.

Luci continued to moan. She didn't want to believe any of this was real. Her eyes slowly roamed the room, the stainless steel railings, the wires, the monitors.

"Where are my mom and dad? I need to find them," she said, panicked, trying to rip out the lines that were attached to her monitors, and kicking the sheets off.

Holding Luci down to replace the wires, the nurse said, "I understand, but, right now, Luci you need to stay in bed until the doctor can check your leg and head. If she says it's okay, we can take all the monitors off, but you need to stay still for just a little longer."

"Please let me get up. My leg and my head only hurt a little. I need to see my mom and dad," Luci pleaded.

The nurse walked over to the closet and came back with Teddy. She smoothed Luci's hair away from her face as she handed the precious bear over.

Luci held the stuffed bear tightly in her arms.

"Your teddy bear had a little hole in his toe, so I took him to the break room with me and patched him up. Now, he's as good as new. See where the hole was?"

Ignoring the nurse, Luci began to cry. "Where are my mom and dad?" She suspected something was very wrong, but she didn't want to believe anything bad had happened to them.

"You have the most beautiful green eyes, Luci," said the nurse, "I'll tell the doctor you're awake."

A few minutes later, a petite brunette, entered Luci's hospital room holding a chart. She touched her arm. "You were in a very bad car accident," she said, sitting down on the edge of Luci's bed. "My name is Dr Jones I am so sorry honey, but your mom and dad didn't make it. I'm so very sorry."

Luci felt her soul rip out of her body. She'd never felt so alone. She was scared and her head hurt so badly. She couldn't stop the tears leaking out of her eyes. Her breathing sped up and lurched out of bed in search of her parents. The doctor and nurse grabbed Luci and held her by her arms, forcing her back onto the bed. The nurse quickly stuck a needle in her arm, assuring her in a soothing voice that she'd feel better soon. Luci quieted down, clutching her teddy and crying silently into his fur. The bear was the last thing her mommy had given her. Soon, the drug took effect and she drifted off to sleep.

The next day, the nurse who had fixed Luci's teddy bear came into her room, bringing a woman wearing a black habit.

"Luci, I'd like to introduce you to Sister Clara. She is going to visit you while you get better. Our social worker will look for your Uncle Nick and your mother's parents. You mentioned their names to the firefighter who brought you in."

Looking Sister Clara over, Luci remarked, "Why are you wearing sandals?"

"Women have played many roles over the centuries. I wear these in remembrance of them," explained Sister Clara.

Luci did not say another word. She was exhausted and had a horrible ache tearing her insides out.

"It's okay, Luci. I'm here if you need me. You don't have to talk if you don't want to. I'll just sit in the corner chair and, if you need anything, I'll get it for you."

Hour after hour, the nun sat in the chair and said nothing.

The nurse quietly came in to check on Luci. "How are you doing?"

Luci ignored her. As she rocked and watched over Luci, she thought of how the Wheel of Fortune in the tarot cards was temporary. Luci's family, who were members of the Cathars, had sent her to watch over Luci. Sister Clara had infiltrated the Catholic Church long ago and had found its Catholic school where Luci would soon be sent.

Sister Clara would be able to continue watching over Luci. Luci would face many moral choices and she was just a temporary presence in her life.

The Cathars believed in cards they refer to as tarot. They represent their history. They are not fortune-telling cards as people now believe. Long ago, gypsies would pass them at their camps to spread the word about the Cathar families. Sister Clara was a Magician in the tarot cards, coupled with the Wheel. That was why she had been chosen for this position. Her cards equaled Force. For now, she sat in her chair knitting, while biding her time until Luci's strength recovered. Others would come soon to take her place.

Luci did not speak to her. Not a word. She only held her bear close, staring out the window into the Del Monte forest. She stared at a tree, the leaves rustling in the wind. A red woodpecker, its head bobbing, repeatedly punched holes into the bark of another tree.

Luci never moved. She lay still on the clean white sheets, as if she had died along with her parents. Sister Clara felt a sense of urgency, a premonition of something to come. It frightened her.

Nurses came and went during their daily shifts, as did Luci's doctor to check on her leg.

A week later, a social worker came and told Luci they hadn't found her relatives yet, but they would keep looking. Luci didn't even look at her. Instead, she continued staring at the tree outside that had begun to sprout gold and orange leaves. Somehow, it had survived the storm they'd had the week before. The storms in Monterey could be fierce, knocking over a number of trees. When walking in the Del Monte forest, people always had to be careful.

Luci's parents were taken away and a dark storm rained down. Things would never be the same for Luci, or for Sister Clara.

Esclarmonde's Diary

Light of the World

December, 1200

I lived in Occitan, a country divided between the Crown of Aragon
and the Country of Toulouse. The people were Albigensian because of the 1176 Church Council held near Albi that had declared
the Cathar doctrine heretical. The country had sophisticated and
powerful nobles who resented papal authority and the taxes the
church weighed upon all the people of Occitan to protect the
Cathars.

My Aunt Corba told me that Raimond Roger, known as the
Count de Foix and the great hero of the south, was my father – a
man who, in his youth, had romanced and won the hand of
Etienette de Penautier, the prettiest woman in the Languedoc. He
was remembered by his subjects as "Raymond Drut" or "Raymond the Beloved," the people had great respect for him. In the
autumn, the count got lost during a hunting party. Tired and drunk
from the day, he'd spotted a building with high white walls and
banged on its gate to demand entrance. He'd been surprised when
a pretty abbess, Na Ermingarda, had come to the door.

Opening the door just enough to see who was there, Na had
explained that no man was allowed in the abbey.

Forcing the door open, the count had slurred, "This is my land,
abbess, and if you and the other nuns want to keep living here, then
you will let me stay the night."

Na had reluctantly agreed. She'd turned to leave for evening
prayers when Raymond grabbed her roughly, threw her down on
the dirt floor, ripped her habit, and raised her skirts. He clamped
his hand on her mouth to prevent her from screaming and thrust
his fingers deep inside her.

"My, oh my. She's a virgin," he'd laughed.

Untying the rope that held his pants up, he raised his penis out of his pants. His only misdeed would be against God since the abbess was the bride of Christ. No crime would be committed against the virgin abbess according to the rules of the land.

"I see that I need a little help, madam, because of all the ale I have drunk," the count had said.

Taking his hand from her face, he pushed her down to her knees and thrust his penis into her mouth. Trying to scream and pull away only made it worse for Na.

"I will slit your throat and anyone else I find here if you don't do as I command," the count whispered.

Na could only comply. There were many nuns in the chapel whom she had to protect. Throwing her onto her back, then, he'd mounted her, lifting her gown and thrusting himself deep inside her. She'd grasped him tightly around his back as he moved in and out of her, spilling his seed inside. Drunk as he was, there was no stopping him. He then threw Na onto her stomach. With dirty fingers holding her down, he pushed himself deeper and deeper until she bled. Finally, exhausted, he rolled off her and passed out.

He'd raped her in a drunken state and never thought to hear from her again, Esclarmonde thought, vowing she would never let this happen to her.

The next morning, he'd drawn a picture with a chalky substance on a stone, a relief of two knights on a horse, Sigillum Militum Christi, the sign of the Knights Templar, a seal of the Warrior for Christ. Without another thought of the abbess he'd raped, he'd mounted his steed and ridden away, not knowing that he had impregnated her, Esclarmonde's mother.

After a few months, she'd begun to show her pregnancy and, because of her position at the nunnery, she'd left to return home to her family. It had been a long and arduous journey to her village. Na was exhausted and ashamed of what had befallen her. Her family took her in, but her fellow citizens shunned her. In distress, she gave birth early to twins, a boy she named Loup and a girl, Esclarmonde.

Weakened by the shame of the pregnancy and the journey to her parents' home, Na Ermingarda died giving birth. The twins were cared for by a wet nurse.

Because Na's parents had been too old and were unable to afford to raise two children, I, Esclarmonde and my brother were sent to Raymond de Foix's court. The servants and most of my father's family ostracized us. When my brother Loup was five, they'd sent him off to a monastery to receive an education befitting a person of his station. They sequestered me in an octagonal tower on my father's Belpech estate. The count's retainer and my Aunt Corba cared for me. Corba was a Prefect who initiated me into the ways of the Cathars.

My aunt raised me as if I were her own child. As a young girl I had been impetuous, wild, and angry. I'd hated my father for separating me from my brother and I'd hated that my mother had died because of him. One night, I left the castle for a swim after everyone had fallen asleep.

I saw Brother Robert who was returning from Saint-Antonin Abbey where my aunt had sent him to collect a precious artefact. He'd told Aunt Corba later that he heard strange noises and had become startled. Cautiously, he continued on and spotted a fox that sat right before his horse. At the end of the long road, he saw a young naked girl swimming in a hot spring. She rose out of the water, steam emanating from her body. Her skin was not red as it should have been, but the color of alabaster. I saw Brother Robert hungrily gazing at me and my nakedness. I laughed loudly in derision and he'd quickly ridden away in embarrassment.

That evening when he'd arrived at the castle keep, he'd asked for a private meeting with Aunt Corba. He'd told her of seeing a young girl cavorting in the woods while dozens of wild animals surrounded her. He'd told Aunt Corba that it was me and I was evil – a whore like my mother.

"Brother Robert, you have had a long journey from Saint-Antonin Abbey. Please let us get you some sustenance and then some sleep. After that, you can tell me about your adventure in the forest and of my niece," Aunt Corba had responded.

The next morning, Brother Robert had decided it was prudent to say nothing more of what he had seen. Maybe in his delusional state he had seen a witch and not Esclarmonde. If he said more, they might crucify him as a heretic. He was never sure what had happened, but, from that day on, he was wary of Esclarmonde.

Force

We can only be said to be alive in those moments
when our hearts are conscious of our treasures.
~ Thornton Wilder

Present Day

A week later, a nurse helped Luci take a shower, placing a plastic bag over her cast so she wouldn't get her leg wet. Sister Clara left and came back with a bag of children's clothes that adopted children had left behind. Sister Clara helped Luci into a T-shirt and jeans. Another nurse brought a wheelchair into the room.

"Luci, I know you can hear me, honey. The hospital has released you into the care of Sister Clara. She will be taking you to a children's home until your relatives can be located. Don't give up hope, Luci. Sometimes it takes a little longer to find relatives in other countries. We should find your grandparents shortly, but, until then, you must go with Sister Clara. It should only be for a little while," the nurse said gently as she helped Luci into the wheelchair.

Luci remained stone cold, refusing to respond in any way.

Sister Clara wheeled Luci out of the hospital to a van and spoke to her along the way about the number XI card of the tarot, the Force card. "This must be kept between us, Luci. It's our secret," she said, placing the card in Luci's hand. "This will keep you strong and on the path you were destined for. Believe in your family and believe that I am here to protect you at all times."

Luci's parents had told her briefly about the Cathar faith versus the Roman Church when they had spoken to her about religion. Looking down, she saw that the card had a picture of a Cathar woman holding the head of a lion and wearing sandals.

Luci wondered then if Sister Clara was a Cathar Prefect because she wore sandals.

"War is coming between now and the past," Sister Clara went on. "Luci, you are in the middle of it and need to prepare for what your distant relative, Corba, had predicted would occur."

Luci was confused and couldn't fully understand why Sister Clara was telling her all of this or how it involved her. She had no previous knowledge of a relative named Corba and was suspicious of everything that was happening to her. She felt her life spinning out of control, as if she were on a Ferris wheel that just wouldn't stop turning.

"In the deck of tarot cards, the one called the High Priestess is holding the head of the lion who was King Louis. The Roman Church was in league with King Louis and they made an allegiance to kill the Knights Templar and their supporters, the Cathars," Sister Clara explained. "The remaining Cathars of today sent me to protect you and to find your grandparents in France to continue the search for a lost artefact."

Luci silently wondered if Sister Clara was losing her mind. Frightened by the woman's babbling, Luci had no idea what any of it had to do with her.

Sister Clara helped Luci into the van and handed her teddy bear to her along with a pair of crutches.

"Luci, your parents have gone to be with God. They are at peace, and now we will care for you until your grandparents or your uncle are located." Luci just looked ahead, and clung to her teddy bear. She couldn't help wondering what was to become of her. She felt guilty that she hadn't died along with her parents. The van passed a road sign that read Gilroy, then turned left and traveled down a bumpy, dirt road that had rows of garlic growing on either side.

The van stopped in front of an old two-storey building. Sister Clara opened Luci's door. The air was pungent with the smell of garlic. Silently, Luci followed the nun toward the door. Looking up, she saw a bunch of other girls staring down at her through their bedroom windows. Another nun came up to Sister Clara, took Luci by the hand, then led her into the foyer.

Leaning over, she whispered, "Be careful of Sister Margarite."

Luci soon came to understand that Sister Margarite was a no-nonsense nun. "Bad things happened every day," she would often say.

It was God's will. There was nothing more to be said. Sister Margarite was plainspoken and to the point.

"We will need to find you some sensible shoes and clothes while you live here," she said. "I'll take you upstairs so you can have some time to yourself. I will be up later to check on you."

Climbing the stairs proved rather difficult with crutches. A quiet girl came up behind Luci. She appeared to be close to Luci in age, had sad brown eyes, and was very skinny – with a forlorn look on her face. "Let me help you carry these upstairs," she said.

Luci was worried the girl might get hurt, but she accepted her offer. "Thank you," she said. "What's your name?"

"Sarah. Where's your room? I'll help you get there, but then I have to go so I don't get into trouble."

"I'm Luci. It's to the left, second door," she said, repeating Sister Margarite's instructions.

"Then I guess we'll be roommates." Sarah helped Luci to their shared room and, with that small gesture, forged a friendship that would last a lifetime.

Sarah disappeared as quickly as she had appeared.

Luci gazed around the two-storey farmhouse. The smells of the field infiltrated every crevice in the old house. It was a pungent smell, but, oddly, it somehow comforted Luci because Sunday nights had always been spaghetti nights at home. Her father loved to put lots of garlic on everyone's plate of noodles.

Her eyes settled on the interior of her new room. She gazed in horror at the ugly metal bed and its coverlet – dingy with yellow and orange flowers. It was nothing like her beautiful princess bedroom at home, with its canopy and fluffy goose-down comforter to keep her warm at night.

She heard the door open and saw Sister Margarite watching her. "I came by to see how you're settling in. You will be getting up each morning at five a.m. for breakfast. Then you will have classes by a choir mistress to learn the text and the Gregorian chanting of the Sacred Office," she informed Luci. "Now, move along."

Sister Margarite remembered her days as a novice when she had not yet submitted to her vows. She attended regular classes like the ones she required of Luci. At one time, she thought she would submit to the divine office. She believed it was her calling, but after what she had witnessed, her job was now to protect the girls.

Luci's mind drifted to her last birthday party with her parents and friends. There'd been cake, ice cream, and a juggling clown. Everyone had been happy, nothing like here.

"Are you listening to me, missy?"

Luci perked up.

"You will have your meals in with the other children who live here," the stern nun continued. "You will attend a private Catholic school on the grounds. You are quite fortunate that Father Del Pierro was at the hospital when you arrived. He has chosen to give you a scholarship to our school. However, after your studies, there will be plenty of work on the land for you to do to make up for his generosity. You will sleep over there in that bed. The dresser up against the wall and to the left is yours. The drawers stick, so grab some WD40 from the pantry and it will be good as new."

Luci didn't think the room, bed, or drawers could ever be "good as new," even if they took a blow-torch to it all. Someone else now controlled her life. She wanted to run away, but she wouldn't get far with a broken leg. She just wanted to cry. She would never succumb to tears in front of this nun or anyone else ever again.

"You will wear the clothes and shoes that have been provided. You will have no more need for the frilly dress in the bag you came from the hospital with and, really, Luci, you are far too old to be holding onto a teddy bear," Sister Margarite disciplined her.

The nun reached out to take the teddy bear out of Luci's arms. Panicked, Luci backed up, but the nun kept coming at her. Luci was looking for a direction to run to get away from the nun's clutching hands when she bumped into Sister Clara just outside the bedroom door.

"Let her have the bear, Sister Margarite," Sister Clara insisted. "That's all that she has left of her family."

"Thank you, Sister Clara, for your insight," Sister Margarite reluctantly admitted. "Ahh, here you are back and late again, aren't you, Sarah? Please tuck in your shirt and straighten up your skirt, young lady. What have you been doing?"

"I'm sorry, Sister. I was studying with Father Del Pierro."

Sister Margarite was afraid of the Father. She'd heard rumors of his sinful ways and what he might be doing to the girls. He'd told her to mind her own business on many occasions. Moreover, she didn't want to cause another scene because of a young girl arriving in disarray.

"As you know, you will be sharing a room with Luci," Sister Margarite said to Sarah. "Her parents are dead, like your mother." Still angry at Sister Clara's reprimand about the bear, the nun began to close the bedroom door. As an afterthought, she said, "Sarah will help you learn the rules of the house and your responsibilities, Luci. Since you won't answer me, maybe we should treat you like you're deaf and dumb." She turned swiftly and walked out.

Luci stared at Sarah. The disheveled Sarah looked as broken as Luci felt. Sarah walked over to her side of the room, laid on the bed, and cried. Her cropped, mousy, brown hair, masked the tears falling down her red swollen face. Luci picked up her crutches, hobbled over to Sarah's bed, and put her arms around Sarah's shoulders until she stopped crying.

Something was wrong in this place.

Learning the ropes

To live is the rarest thing in the world.
Most people exist, that is all.
~ Oscar Wilde

Present Day
Drying her eyes, Sarah sat up and took Luci's hand. "Thank you," she said without explaining on why she was crying. "I'll show you where the bathroom is so we can wash up before dinner."

"Are you okay?" Luci asked, afraid that Sarah was in some sort of trouble.

Sarah quickly said, "Let's forget about it and go eat. Don't talk during dinner, or we'll all get into trouble." Sarah led Luci to the dining room.

"Why?" Luci hadn't spoken in a week, since she learned of the death of her parents, but now she wanted to know why she couldn't talk at dinner.

"Just don't," Sarah warned again.

Luci had never been one to be afraid of much, but now, alone, she was terrified. Sarah held her hand, guided her to a bench in the dining room, then sat down next to her. An older girl bumped Sarah off the bench and onto the floor. All the girls laughed. Luci reached down to help Sarah up. The older girl warned Luci, "You help her and we'll hurt you, get it?"

Luci got up from the bench and helped Sarah up. It was difficult because of her broken leg, but she wasn't about to leave her new friend. The girls in the dining room gasped in horror.

"You'll be sorry you did that, baby," warned the girl.

Sarah and Luci left the dining room, hand-in-hand, and walked to their room.

"Why did that girl knock you down?"

"My father is important and Father Del Pierro likes to make sure that I know I am now under his control. Janet does his dirty work for him."

"Where is your father?"

"He is out of the country and my mother is gone. He sent me here to learn."

"Is there anyone we can report her to?"

"It would only make things worse," Sarah responded.

Sarah and Luci became best friends who shared their hopes and dreams. They worked in the garden together and helped each other with homework. At times, Sarah would disappear and later return, crying. Luci didn't question Sarah, but knew her friend was being hurt by someone. Someday, Luci knew, Sarah would tell her what was happening, but she also knew that she couldn't outright ask. Whatever it was, it was terrible. Luci was afraid for Sarah, but she didn't want to hurt her friend by prying.

"In God's time," the nuns always said.

Maybe this was one of those times.

† † †

The days were long, the school work hard, but out in the garden, Luci could dream about her parents, her home, and how life had been. She dreamed of her grandparents or her uncle coming to take her away from here. She didn't want to leave Sarah behind, though, and hoped her family would take Sarah, too. Luci wanted to share her room at home, her friends at her old school, and her former life with her new friend. She felt calmed by these dreams.

All the orphan girls had chores. As soon as the doctor removed Luci's cast, she was sent to the garden to pull the garlic out of the ground to sell to local stores. Luci actually enjoyed it. The only downside was working with Sister Margarite, whose hands were gnarled and arthritic. Sister Margarite pulled a few weeds but was always prying into her business or Sarah's. Luci quit listening to her and just enjoyed being outside. She felt she was paying back the church's orphanage by bringing in money for food and clothes for all the kids. Gardening kept her mind off her own troubles and gave her something positive to focus on.

Janet and her friends were walking toward them as they lugged a basket full of garlic back to the barn.

Pushing Luci to the ground, she sneered and said, "You're a kiss-ass. Keep away from the slut."

"Why did you do that to me, and what do you mean?" Luci screamed.

"You think you're so great. You're not; you're just like us. You're an orphan and no one loves you or is going to come and take you away from here."

"Leave me alone, Janet," Luci retorted.

The other kids gathered around them.

"Hit her," they chanted. "She's such a sissy with her teddy bear. Knock her out."

† † †

In the distance, Sister Clara watched the scene building up. The Phoenix in the tarot cards was beginning to rise, she thought.

† † †

Slowly getting up from the ground, Luci purposely dusted herself off, and calmly said to Janet, "Don't do that again or you'll be sorry."

Janet ignored her and knocked Luci down again. The kids all laughed. Luci rolled and kicked her legs out, hitting Janet's legs with such force it knocked her into the mud. Luci jumped on top of Janet, slugged her on the nose, in her chest, then added a quick punch to the stomach. Out of the corner of her eye, she saw Sister

Clara running toward them, but before she could reach them, Luci jumped up off Janet and kicked her in the ribs. Bending down to where Janet lay sprawled on the ground, she grabbed Janet's shirt and said, "I warned you. Don't do it again or I promise I will kill you."

Janet got up and ran to the house, crying for Father Del Pierro. Luci glared at the other children as they looked at their shoes and walked away.

Luci ambled to her room where she found Sarah sitting on her bed listening to a song by Miley Cyrus. Luci figured Father Del Pierro would summon her to his office for her behavior. She didn't know what to expect and she was frightened.

"You're bleeding, Luci. Let me get a cloth to clean your face," Sarah said, jumping off her bed.

"Sarah, why don't the other kids don't like us?"

Sarah's face went blank and she said nothing. She retrieved a cloth from the bathroom and cleaned Luci's face. "You had a nice family. Most of us here never had a family at all. Maybe that's why."

"But we're all in the same situation, Sarah."

"I don't think so. Some of us are treated differently than others."

"Why's that?" Luci asked, trying to figure out what was really behind all this.

"Del Pierro," Sarah answered. "Now let it go. We have to get some sleep because tomorrow is a big day."

The next day, Luci went into the garlic field with Sarah as usual to meet up with Sister Margarite. They didn't see her, but began pulling the garlic anyway. It didn't take long before Luci and Sarah were hot and dirty. They walked over to the water faucet near the outside restroom and found Sister Clara stumbling around. She had a deep cut to the back of her head and she was bleeding profusely. Luci helped Sister Clara lay down, grabbed her own dress fiercely and tore it apart to try and stop the bleeding, but it just wouldn't stop. Her hands were covered in Sister Clara's blood. She began to cry.

"Luci, snap out of it, run to the house and get help!" Sarah screamed.

"I'll be right back Sister Clara," Luci jumped up, running as fast as she could to get help. She found Sister Margarite, and the two raced back and found Sarah kneeling next to Sister Clara, she had died before help had arrived. Her body lay on the ground, her head covered in blood. Sarah knelt next to her, tears streaming down on her cheeks.

An ambulance arrived, its wailing siren reminding Luci of the accident. Father Del Pierro came rushing over. They told all the children to go to their rooms.

Sister Clara

In three words I can sum up everything I've learned about life:
it goes on.
~ Robert Frost

When Luci and Sarah opened the door to their room, all their belongings were on the floor, along with an envelope containing a tarot card. It was the High Priestess card, and on the back was a name: Luci. The envelope was addressed to Sister Clara and the return address was from France. Sarah slipped the card into her pocket when Luci wasn't looking, and they began putting away the little belongings she had.

Could this be related to Sister Clara's death? Sarah wondered, as she put her underclothes back in drawers.

"If it is, for what reason?" Luci asked

"I have no idea. I don't have anything of value, do you?" Sarah asked.

"Me? Hardly," Luci said, half-smiling. "Did Sister Clara say anything to you before she passed away?"

"She told me to be careful and to watch over you. She loved both of us and always tried to protect us."

Luci would never forget Sister Clara. Sister Clara had always been there for her after the death of her parents, she didn't know what to do. She was all alone again. Another accident, Luci thought to herself. Just like her parents had been. She wouldn't forget this.

Luci recalled her mother telling her that, in revenge, as in life, every action had an equal and opposite reaction. The guilty would always fail; the honorable would survive to fight another day.

From that day on, Luci stayed away from the other kids. They always seemed to want to hurt her and went out of their way to bump her or push her down. In front of them, she acted and talked tough, but, in reality, that wasn't who she was. That was when she found an outlet to other worlds in the library. She read all the books, including the Bible. All the sisters were impressed with the amount of knowledge Luci picked up from her studies and from the extra readings on St Paul, Jesus, Thomas, Mary, and John the Divine. She could quote excerpts from the Bible and loved the passages, particularly from the Old Testament

† † †

Sister Margarite had been different since the death of Sister Clara. She'd been in the kitchen looking over the meals that were being prepared for the girls that day. To her horror, she saw Father Del Pierro come up behind Sister Clara, hit her in the head with a rock, then take her out to the garden. She'd had no choice, she said, but to stay quiet. The school was her only home and she needed to protect the children as best she could.

She entered the library and saw Luci studying, "Be careful, Luci. Father Del Pierro is watching you and Sarah both. I will try to find a way to get you away from here, I'll write a letter to a friend of mine," she said.

Luci didn't know what to think. Strange things seemed to be happening around her and Sarah, but Luci didn't know why.

† † †

That night, Sister Margarite wrote to Sister Evangeline who lived near the Vatican. She told her of Sister Clara's efforts to try to find Luci's grandparents and the apparent mistreatment of Luci and Sarah by Father Del Pierro. She was taking a huge risk by finally exposing these truths.

Her friend told her she would help but they would have to do it in secret. Things were happening in the Vatican that she didn't completely understand. There was a power struggle going on between two elements in the Vatican. Cardinal Saachio was on one side and had many friends, one of whom was Father Del Pierro.

"Dear Sister Evangeline," she wrote back, "please say nothing. No good will come of this. Protect the children. We will find Luci's grandparents."

Spring faded and summer was upon the school. Life didn't seem to exist outside the farmhouse. Frightened by the death of Sister Clara, Luci and Sarah stayed close to the school and away from the girls and Father Del Pierro.

On a bright summer day, Luci spotted Sister Margarite walking toward her and Sarah as they harvested the garlic.

"I have some good news for you, Luci. Your grandparents have been found," she said in a whisper. "They are waiting to see you. They're here to take you back to your home. Don't look so concerned, Luci, they are kind people and want you to know that you are not alone anymore. Please follow me," she said gently.

Luci wasn't sure she wanted to see them. After so long, she didn't know what to think. However, she didn't want to stay at the orphanage any longer. She was torn because she didn't want to leave Sarah behind.

"Come with me, Sarah," she said.

"I'll be okay, Luci. Go ahead and see your family."

Reluctantly, Luci left with Sister Margarite. She remembered how her mom spoke of her parents, telling Luci that they were kind and gentle and how much she missed them. Her mom had promised a trip to France one day to see the Pyrenees Mountains and Montsegur, where her family had lived for centuries and where they would visit her parents. Luci had been excited about meeting her relatives, but things had changed. Now, she didn't know what she wanted. What if she didn't like them? What if they hated her?

"Just give them a chance, Luci. They really want to be here with you," Sister Margarite said.

With her head down, Luci hesitantly walked toward Father Del Pierro's office. Sister Margarite knocked on the door, and Luci and the nun entered. Two elderly people sat, holding hands, looking timidly at Luci.

"Luci, these are your grandparents, Anna and Lou."

Luci's grandmother hesitated only a moment, then walked right over to Luci and kissed her cheek.

"*Mon cher, nous somme vos grands-parents* – oh, I'm sorry. We are your grandparents. Sometimes we slip into French. Please excuse us. We have been living in France for a very long time. Your mama sent us pictures of you while you were growing up. You are so beautiful. You look just like her when she was a child. Here, I brought you a locket of hers and I want you to have it." Her grandmother stroked Luci's hair, just as her mother had long ago.

Luci carefully put the silver chain around her neck. Looking inside, she saw a picture of her mother, a thread to the past she thought she had lost.

"Luci," her grandfather said. "We are so sorry that it has taken us so long to find you under these conditions. We want to take you back to your home where we can all live together in the place you shared with your mom and dad."

Luci honestly didn't know what to make of all of this. She wanted her mom and dad. She didn't know these people. She was scared and confused.

Luci's grandparents took her by her hand. As they were walking down the stairs, Luci noticed her grandfather limped. She saw Sarah running toward her. Luci was afraid Sarah would get into trouble, but Sister Margarite looked the other way.

"You almost forgot your bear, Luci."

Luci hugged Sarah. She didn't want to leave her all alone. "I'll do all I can so that you can come live with us, Sarah," she promised. Luci turned away from Sarah and looked hopefully at her grandparents, "Can you adopt Sarah?"

"Thank you, Luci, maybe one day I'll get to come and visit you," Sarah said. "I will miss you, Luci, as well," said Sarah.

Father Del Pierro looked down from the balcony. Sarah turned to walk upstairs and caught just a glimpse of him hiding behind the curtains.

It was a shame Luci was leaving, he thought. She wouldn't be if it weren't for that meddling bitch, Sister Clara. A letter must have gotten through to France. He had been snagging them since Luci's arrival from the outgoing mail.

† † †

Sister Margarite handed Luci a cloth bag that held her belongings. Inside was the dress that Uncle Nick had given her the day her parents had died. Looking up at her grandparents, she saw that her grandfather's eyes had tears in them. Luci stretched out her hand and quietly slipped it into his.

Looking at his beautiful granddaughter, he said, "We are family, Luci. You are a de Foix and a Cathar from Montsegur, France. We will be together, and we will keep you safe."

Luci wasn't sure what a Cathar was. She'd heard Sister Clara and her parents mention it before, but she didn't know what it meant. Nothing mattered now because she was going home, and her grandfather promised she would be safe.

"Luci, in life, all things inevitably change. The lesson in this is that the spiritual person is required to choose goodness and, in this way, he prevents himself from being drawn downward into the realm of base animal instincts. Your wheel of fortune, your destiny, has changed. You will have happiness, contentment, and love."

What do these words mean? Luci wondered as she walked with her grandparents out the front door of the orphanage and opened the door of a red Cadillac to face her new life.

Esclarmonde's Diary

April, 1201
Folques, a traveling troubadour, had come to my uncle's castle on many occasions for the advancement of poetry and love. Tonight there was to be a grand party and all the troubadours of high standing would be there.

Cautiously advancing toward me, Folques said, "To be in love is to reach heaven through my Lady Esclarmonde."

Folques was one of the great troubadours in my uncle's kingdom and we were fortunate to have him grace our castle. He was a womanizer of ill-repute and his admiration for me was scandalous. If the church heard of it, my soul would be in jeopardy. Handsome, full of himself, dangerous, but at the same time, very exciting. He was trouble, for sure.

Folques had been born to wealthy parents – merchants – in the year 1200. When he reached the age of twenty, he left for the City of Occitan to become a juggler, minstrel, and the troubadour for which he became admired. His reputation had grown as he'd traveled through Languedoc, performing for the courts of Raymond V of Toulouse and my uncle Raimond-Roger of Foix. But, on that same evening, I met and fell in love with a Knight Templar – Guilhelm. I did not respond to Folques' advances after that day and I did not hear of him again until she saw him in Montsegur.

I discovered he had given up being a troubadour after I declined his affections. He had moved on to become one of the most influential representatives of the church at the local level. Now a bishop, he was given the greatest legal authority and had the power to make life and death decisions.

Folques later joined the Cistercian order, fighting alongside the French and Roman Church during the Albigensian Crusade. He raised his own band of followers against the Cathars, possibly out of spite, under the name of The Order of Brotherhood, seeking revenge against heretics like me.

The Knight

Those who don't believe in magic will never find it.
~ Roald Dahl

Present Day
On the drive back to Luci's home that she had once shared with her parents, her grandfather described her family's life in Montsegur. He told her about the people of their homeland, the beautiful valleys where the green of spring gave way to the gold of summer, and the copper of autumn gave way to the gray of winter. She drifted away to a time where she was happy with her mom and dad.

She barely listened as he spoke about the Cathars, Montsegur, and France. She laid her head back on the seat of the car, feeling alienated; these people were strangers who had never been a part of her life.

Arriving home, she couldn't wait to revisit her room. A woman with bleached-blonde hair opened the door and smiled. "Hello, Luci. Your grandparents have told me so much about you. You are as beautiful as your mama. My name is Gabby. I'm looking forward to being here with you and your grandparents. Your home is quite beautiful."

"Thank you, Gabby," Luci said, instantly mistrusting the woman who seemed to like her home as much as Luci did. Maybe more.

"Luci, we have a surprise waiting for you," her grandfather said as she turned and saw him holding out an Australian Shepherd puppy.

Luci stretched out her arms. She took the little fuzzball from her grandfather and held her close. She felt safe being home, and now she had grandparents who were trying to make her feel a part of them. When Luci looked up, the puppy was licking her tears away. She didn't realize she'd been crying. Luci squeezed the dog tight to her, never wanting to let her go.

"Thank you so much. She's so beautiful."

"Your mother and father told us long ago how much you wanted a puppy, and now she will keep you safe. You may keep her in your room if you like," her grandfather said.

Luci took her puppy into her bedroom and the two of them lay down together on her bed.

"I think I will name you Sophia," she said.

Sophia snuggled up close, licking Luci's face.

†††

The next day, Luci's grandparents took her back to her old school where her friends and even the principal came out to greet her. Being back felt right. The principal took her to the classroom where she introduced her to her new teacher, and her teacher, in turn, presented her to her classmates. Many she knew from before, and she fell right back into the rhythm of her old life. The only part that was missing were her parents and Sarah.

Luci hadn't heard from Sarah in weeks, and she worried about her and her safety there. Her last letter was frightening. Sister

Margarite had accidentlly fallen down the stairs. The paramedic had said her heart had just stopped.

Luci felt huge regret in judging Sister Margarite so harshly in the beginning and felt sad at her death. She hoped that Sarah would be okay and wrote her that same day.

† † †

Luci enjoyed school and was very active on the cheerleading squad, and when she graduated into the sixth grade, she became the school class president.

Every day, Gabby would pick her up from school and drive her to a Kung Fu studio. She enjoyed the hard work and discipline that she put into her lessons, as well as being able to release all her anger. Her sifu worked with her. He taught her the yin and yang of the movements of the five animals. She learned the Tiger, Dragon, Crane, Snake, and Leopard.

Her sifu was impressed with his student, so young and yet so determined, he thought. Whatever exercise he put before the class, Luci was the first to try it and to master it. Most American kids wouldn't tolerate the discipline expected out of the Chinese White Lotus System of Kung Fu, but Luci did, she thrived in it.

That very first day she had walked into the studio with her grandparents her head held high, contemplative, like this was her mission. First-month students were expected to stand in a horse stance for fifteen minutes. It was like sitting in a chair, knees bent, without a chair to sit on. Sifu could see sweat dripping off the faces of the new students. Many would fall to the ground. Luci stood in the stance, determination written on her face. Every exercise he put before her, she did without complaint, and she was like no student he had had before.

"Luci, you are my best student," he told her one day. "You never say anything and you never complain when you get hit in your floor matches with other students."

"Yes, sifu."

No one knew that Luci had looked up an old local newspaper story about the accident that killed her parents on the Internet. She found out that investigators had discovered someone had cut the brake lines in the Oldsmobile. In the back of Luci's mind, she was determined to find out who killed her parents, and make them pay.

Grief occurs in five stages: denial, anger, bargaining, depression, and, finally, acceptance. For her, grief was a life sentence without parole. She would never forgive and she would always remember the death of her parents until the person who killed them was lying at her feet – dead. Until then, she would practise and she would learn from her sifu.

One day, her sifu introduced her to Sher Lew. He was a Master of the White Lotus system and taught her meditation and weaponry. She became proficient in the double axes, and was a strong competitor in the discipline of Kung Fu.

To Luci, he was her knight. He taught her to be independent, to be merciless in a fighting match, but kind to those outside the ring. In every life, there came a day of reckoning, and, for Luci the fighting arena was where she meted out her revenge for Sister Clara, Sister Margarite, and her parents.

"Luci, I am going to take you and your classmates to Long Beach for an international tournament that's held every year," Sher Lew said. "All of you are ready to compete against other schools in the Chinese system."

Two weeks later, Sifu Lew's students boarded a bus for Long Beach. It was an incredible experience. There were people she had only dreamed of meeting: Curtis Leong, Doug Wong, Brendan Lai, Chuck Norris and all of their students.

Luci fought like a tiger in every match. She would not let her school down, and she would honor her teacher. She would not lose. All of her anger focused on one thing: avenging the death of her parents. In her first match, she competed against a boy about her age named Max. He had black hair and blue eyes, and smirked at her.

Well, she thought, she would wipe that look off his face before the end of the match.

The combatants entered the center of the floor mat. Everyone in the auditorium watched as the competitors bowed to each other and the judges. The boy struck Luci first with his red protective gloves and punched her hard in the face. His teammates laughed and cheered him on.

Luci got up off the floor. The judge gestured for the match to continue. She waited for Max to come to her. He walked toward her with confidence, gloves up, ready to punch her again. Luci jumped into the air, doing a roundhouse kick right into his face. His nose began to bleed. No one was laughing now.

She needed another point to win the match. They stood across from one another. Max was angry. He charged her. *You should never lose your temper in a fight*, she thought. She dropped to the floor and kicked his legs out from under him.

Max fell to the floor in agony.

Luci got up, extending her hand to him. He took her hand and smiled. The better person had beaten him. They bowed to each other, then to the judges to signal the end of the match.

Luci beat opponent after opponent. No one had the pent-up anger that she had, or the will to win at any cost.

At the end of the three-day event, Luci was the overall winner. Chuck Norris, a legend in karate, gave her the silver trophy. She bowed to him in thanks, walked over to her sifu, and handed him the prize.

"This is yours, Sifu Lew."

Sifu Lew bowed in respect to his student and her mastery of the arts.

"Luci, always remember to exploit your opponent's weakness in seeking your revenge."

† † †

On the way home after collecting five tournament trophies, Luci's grandparents broke the news to her. "Luci, we have decided that this is your last tournament."

"Why? I have become so good. I want to continue, please."

"You have become too much of a warrior. You need to be tempered with another skill," her grandfather told her.

Luci loved her grandparents, but they were wrong. She felt someone was watching her and she needed to be prepared. In secret, she would continue her Kung Fu lessons. She would get her revenge on the people who killed her parents. Sifu Lew had told her that before embarking on revenge, one must dig two graves. She didn't plan on being in that second grave.

Esclarmonde's Diary

January, 1201

I gazed out the window in the castle of my relative, Raymond IV, and watched in fascination as the people gathered for the feast of St Magdalene's Day. Women wore gowns with long, tight sleeves and a narrow belt. Over this, they wore the cyclas – a sleeveless surcoat. The more affluent women wore embroidery, with their mantle – held in place by a cord across the chest – lined with fur. Suddenly, a piercing cry came from the ramparts. I heard someone shout from the crowd, "They are attacking us!"

Many of the citizens of Beziers rushed to the ramparts. I watched in horror as thousands of Roman legion soldiers came marching toward the castle from the banks of the Orb. The northern army paraded across the valley with banners from Auvergne, Burgundy, and Limousine. There was even a flag from Germany at the lead, a golden rampant lion on a red field emblazoned on it. Simon de Montfort's herald led the Cistercians and their towering crucifixes of Pope Innocent's III's rage against the Cathars during the Albignesian War. I knew De Montfort. He was evil and out to kill every Cathar, but he wanted me most of all to make an example of and learn the information I held sacred. They were surely after the treasure of the Cathars.

To my horror, I watched in disbelief as the men and women of the castle, after a day of waiting and watching the army parade outside the castle, worked themselves into a rage and stormed out of the protection of the castle, leaving the drawbridge open.

"Our knights cower behind the walls of safety," cried a crazed farmer, dressed in kirtle with a belt. He had a slit up the center of the front so he could move with more ease as he pulled a sword from his belt. "The Franks laid waste to my village and killed my wife and child. I will have my revenge!" he screamed as he stormed out.

The Roman soldiers laughed at the peasants of Beziers. One of the northerners with face scars, from the wars he'd fought, strode onto the drawbridge and challenged the farmer.

The Occitans swarmed the northerner and threw him over the bridge into the treacherous rapids below. I could see the Roman soldiers held sticks and cudgels, and the two groups collided in a fierce battle at the first light of dawn.

Two men came running into the fray, Almaric, a bishop of Rome and Folques, a man I had not laid eyes upon in many years. The northern men gained access to the castle, and Almaric screamed, "Don't allow the fools back in!"

I watched as the northerners dragged half-naked women from their homes and threw babies out the windows. The cathedral priest knelt before the onslaught with his crucifix held high, reminding the northerners of Christ's pacifism. A Frank with an axe sliced the priest's scalp open with one stroke. The priest dropped to the ground. The crucifix lay in the dirt as the men trampled over it.

Folques spotted me watching from above and, to my horror, recognized me. "Ten gold pieces will be given to the man who brings me that woman alive," he said, pointing at me.

One of the knights of our castle came to my rescue and we fled down the rampart. A frantic pealing of bells called the survivors toward the protection of the city's two churches. I left the knight and ran to St Nazaire, but there were so many Occitans inside that they threw the corpses from its towers. A prefect reached out to pull me to safety.

"It is time, dear one. Darkness is surrounding the lands. Malice is in the air, an evil that will destroy and corrupt all that is true and good. You must escape and get to your Aunt Corba," he told me just before they pulled me back into the mob.

A man with half an ear started tearing at my robe. "I know who you are. You're worth ten shillings."

His head snapped back violently. The knight had found me again. He was in black armor with a red cross emblazoned across his chest. He circled his horse around my attacker. The man lunged for the knight's horse's reins.

"Getch yer own bitch!" he shouted.

Denied a full arc for his sword, the crusader pounded on the man's head until he let me go. I staggered toward the cathedral. The crusaders charged past me and kicked in the door from the nave. Blood oozed down the steps. The church reeked of blood, urine, and vomit. Old men, women, children, invalids ... The northern knights had spared no one. I stood in shock and horror, looking at all the people of Beziers murdered by the knights.

The crusader in black had killed the knight who was about to grab me. Wetness splashed against my face. I opened my eyes in horror. A man's head had been split open. His brains covered my face and trickled down my tattered dress. The Templar reached down and hoisted me onto his horse. He whispered to me. It was Guilhelm. The last sounds I heard before passing out were the screams of my fellow Occitans jumping to their deaths from the cathedral's tower.

The Judgment

Do not follow where the path leads,
Rather, go where there is no path
And leave a trail.
~ Ralph Waldo Emerson

Present Day
Luci and her grandparents shared their passion for horses. They participated in all her horse shows, and Grandpa had owned a ranch in Toulouse, France. Anna, Luci's grandmother, had become an expert equestrian, and her mother had almost made the Olympic team on her Dutch Warmblood. Her grandmother shared a photo album of her mother's horse, Destiny, at the different events they'd competed in. Newspaper clippings that her mother had collected over the years filled a book decorated with ribbons.

To start Luci in riding, her grandparents bought her a Hackney pony, Chili. He was black and had a great disposition for a young girl starting out. Luci would tack Chili up and Sophia would run alongside her wherever she rode on the ranch.

One afternoon, Luci headed for a trail in the walnut grove. One of the girls had spotted a baby fox and she wanted to look at it. Her trainer never let her go outside the property boundary.

"Luci!" he said. "Get back here."

"Caught again, Chili. Okay, Dave, I was just trying to get a peek at the baby fox."

"I know what you were doing, and I told you to always stay on the property so I can watch you. Why aren't you wearing your helmet?"

"Sorry, I'll go get it," Luci said, annoyed that she'd been caught without it.

Running to get her helmet from the tack room, she bumped into the new hired hand at the Waterfalls stable.

"Wow, slow down, little one."

"Sorry. I almost ran you down."

"No problem. And who is this with you?"

"This is my dog, Sophia. Are you new here?"

"Yes, young lady. My name's Reynaldo. I'm originally from the Philippines. I'm a friend of Gabby, your grandparents' caretaker. Your name's Luci, right?"

"Yes, sir," Luci said cautiously.

"Gabby told me she worked for your grandparents and that you took lessons here. She also said that your dog followed you everywhere, so it was easy to figure out," he said with a smile.

"It's nice to meet you, Reynaldo. Oh, here come my grandparents. Let me introduce you to them. This is my grandmother, Anna, short for Madeleine, and my grandfather, Lou, short for Louie. They shortened their names to make it easier for people who aren't French."

Taking his hat off, Reynaldo bowed. "It is a pleasure to meet someone who has such a wonderful granddaughter."

"He is from the Philippines and this is his first day here," Luci said to her grandparents. "Gabby got him the job."

"It is nice to meet you as well, Reynaldo," Luci's grandfather said warily, shaking his hand. "We look forward to seeing you again."

As Reynaldo turned away, he yelled a goodbye to Luci, then casually strolled to the horse barn with a lopsided swagger she had only seen in old John Wayne movies. Luci giggled at the picture she was forming in her head. Her grandparents anxiously watched him.

"Luci, Dave is looking for you. Hurry up because we have to leave. It's almost time to eat dinner, and you need to do your homework before it gets too late."

"You didn't seem to like Reynaldo, Grandfather. Why are you judging him when you don't know him?"

† † †

Once out of sight, Reynaldo thought to himself, *the little girl is growing*. It was time to rise up to Judgment. Her family was Cathar and believed that Jesus was not human, therefore, the crucifixion and resurrection had to be false. This was blasphemous. He needed to get closer, but Dave was going to be a problem. The man spied on Luci while she was on the ranch. Her grandfather could also be a problem. Reynaldo could see in his eyes that the man didn't trust him. Reynaldo remembered the last night that he and Del Pierro had spent in the Philippines. They'd had dinner at Campagnia and had then strolled back through the palm trees to Del Pierro's hotel. Reynaldo loved the Father with all his heart, but he knew that Father Del Pierro was not like him. People in the Philippines had made fun of Reynaldo as a boy. They'd teased him and said he was more like a girl than a man, but Father Del Pierro took care of him. Reynaldo would do anything for Del Pierro. God forgive his soul.

Before he got in his car, Luci's grandfather gazed at Reynaldo. He recognized Reynaldo, that meant Del Pierro had found them. He was still looking for the key. In the Last Judgment, he recalled, the focus shifted from salvation by holy proxy to individual responsibility. It was Lou's job to guard Luci from Del Pierro and The Order. The Gospel of Philip said, "Those who say we must die first and then rise are in error." Rather, we should "receive the resurrection whilst alive." This had been written in the Cathars' text and had been burned along with all other documents from the Cathars.

Sarah

Don't cry because it's over; smile because it happened.
~ Dr Seuss

On the drive home, Luci could barely hold still. Sophia was in the back seat with her. She cuddled the dog and told her grandparents of her trainer, Dave, and his horse.

"Dave said I could ride her tomorrow in the round pen. She is the Saddlebred I told you about. She's a beautiful chestnut mare. He also said I'm doing very well riding Chili, but it's time for me to advance. Thank you for the riding lessons. They mean so much to me. I promise I will not forget to take the garbage out for you every day, Grandma," she rattled on in her excitement.

When they arrived home, Luci gave her grandma a big hug. Darting out of the car with Sophia not far behind, she raced into the house, colliding with Gabby. "Sorry, Gabby. Call me when it's time for dinner. I'll start working on my homework right now."

"Before you leave, Luci, we have someone who would like to see you."

Grabbing a cookie off the kitchen counter, Luci turned around and saw Sarah.

Luci stood dumbfounded. She dropped the cookie on the tiled floor and Sophia gobbled it up. Not caring, the two girls began to scream with delight and talk at the same time. Luci couldn't believe Sarah was standing in front of her. Luci and Sarah ran to one another and hugged each other as if they were never going to let go.

"I have missed you so much, Sarah."

"I've missed you. You mean so much to me. I'm glad we're together again."

Luci's grandmother explained in her broken English that, since the day they'd found Luci, they were determined to adopt Sarah. And with Sister Margarite's help, they did.

"It took a long time, *mon cher*, but, at last, you have your friend and, now, a sister."

"I can't believe it. I have a sister, and we can be together, Sarah!" Luci screamed, jumping up and down.

"I know. I have been hoping and praying for this for so long, Luci. I couldn't call and tell you because we were not sure that the church would let your grandparents adopt me. Sister Margarite helped make it possible. I'm so happy to have a family and you as my sister."

"Grandma, can I show Sarah around? Where will she be sleeping?" Luci asked.

"Grandpa refurbished your father's study and made it into a bedroom while you were at school during the day. We wanted this to be a surprise. When we knew Sarah was coming, we bought a bed. Now, I'll stop talking so you can show Sarah her new home and bedroom."

Squealing with delight, the girls raced upstairs. Luci opened the door to Sarah's new room. It was beautifully decorated in yellows and blues, Sarah's favorite colors. She couldn't believe it. She walked from object to object, touching them, holding onto things as if they were going to disappear. She spied a desk and on it was a brand-new computer. The desk looked tiny, as if swallowed completely.

"Oh, my gosh, is this mine? I can't believe it," Sarah squealed.

"I told them how good you are with processors, Sarah. You love researching everything from the latest games to the newest music."

"There wasn't a CPU like this at the orphanage."

Grandpa knocked on the opened door and brought in Sarah's suitcase. "I heard what you were saying, Sarah, and I think it would be a very good idea if we got you into a school that specializes in PCs after your classes at the local school with Luci."

"But, Grandpa, Sarah could go with me to the barn and ride horses."

"If that is what Sarah wants."

"Luci, I'll go and watch you, but if it's okay with everyone, I really want to go to a technical school," Sarah said with excitement.

Luci was disappointed, but if this was what her new sister wanted, then she would be happy for her. "Come on, Sarah. Let me show you the rest of the house."

They made a full circle around the house and finally made it back to Sarah's new room where she began to unpack her meager belongings.

Luci frowned. "How is the orphanage and how is the bully, Janet?"

"Janet is the same and is always in Father Del Pierro's study. Did you know that Sister Margarite passed away?"

"Yes." It was heartbreaking. In the last months of Luci's stay at the orphanage, Sister Margarite had become a friend.

† † †

Luci's grandfather was happy the girls were together. That night, he got a call from the owner of the stables. Dave, Luci's trainer, was found with a garrotte around his neck, he died in a pig pen.

Walking into the bedroom where his beautiful wife was reading a book, Lou leaned over and whispered softly into his wife's ear, "Shari just called. I think it would be a good time to look for another stable for Luci to ride at."

The next few years flew by fast. Luci's grandparents gave her and Sarah books on anything they wanted to read. These days, Luci was doing a book report on the Cathars, the Knights Templar, the troubadours, and the people of Occitan. Grandfather would be proud of all she had found out.

Luci studied and played hard, but never forgot that someone had killed her parents.

Every Sunday they went to church together at the Gnostic cathedral where Sarah and Luci enjoyed their lessons. One of her grandparents' friends showed them the tarot card of a chariot. "Women were always depicted riding chariots, Luci. This card represents triumph, but it also represents the battle between good and evil. We learn that pride and vanity can bring a person down."

"But what does this have to do with me?" Luci asked.

"The message is that God holds the reins in our lives. Only by giving them over to him can one truly triumph. The message is clear, Luci. You have the ability to choose good over evil. Your chariot will be stuck going nowhere if you live in opposition to the spiritual laws."

"You know that I found out about my parents' death and the way they died, don't you?"

"I was pretty sure you had. I walked by the martial arts studio and I saw you. Your grandparents had forbidden you to go there anymore. I can tell by the way you push yourself in Kung Fu, the weapons, and your horseback riding that, although on the outside you seem sweet and innocent, inside you hold in a deep anger and hatred. You need to let it go, Luci. You're aware of the laws of God. A fire burns within you, and one day if you do not temper yourself, it will consume you. We are all with you, one family, one God."

"I know you mean well," Luci responded, keeping the knowledge that she would never just let it go to herself.

† † †

Her teacher was not sure if Luci really understood the danger she could be in.

Truth

If you tell the truth, you don't have to remember anything
~ Mark Twain

The family gathered around the kitchen table on Luci's eighteenth birthday, celebrating and eating Luci's favorite red velvet cake with extra icing. Her grandfather left the room and returned shortly, handing his granddaughter an envelope that contained a check for a hundred thousand dollars.

Overwhelmed, she asked, "What is this for?"

"We know that you have applied to many colleges, Luci. An envelope from Yale came just the other day for you, remember?"

"Yes, but we can't afford it. Wait. How did you know I was accepted?"

Her grandmother smiled. "My darling Luci, when it is a fat envelope, it can only mean you have a lot of paperwork to fill out. If it is a small envelope, they are not accepting you."

Luci laughed. It was true, and it was the most generous present she had ever received. She threw her arms around her grandparents. She never thought she would have the money to attend Yale.

"Where did you get all this money?"

"We have very good friends in France who want you to succeed in your studies, Luci. They have even put away money in a trust that you will receive later. It is in the Isle of Mann and kept there for when you need it."

"Wow, this is some birthday. Sarah, did you know? What about you?" she asked.

"We were all waiting to find out if you got into Yale, but you tell her, Sarah," Grandpa said.

"I was accepted into MIT with a scholarship. I've been bursting to tell you, but I promised our grandparents that I would wait. I'm so excited for the both of us."

"Oh my goodness, could the day get any better?" Luci exclaimed.

"Wait, Luci, we have one more gift for you." Grandpa handed her a box covered in red paper.

Slowly, Luci unwrapped the box and saw an old book with diary entries from the thirteenth century.

"It's a history about the Cathars and the Knights Templar. A diary written by your ancestor, Esclarmonde d'Alion," Grandpa Lou said.

"When you reach your thirtieth birthday, this book will be delivered to you. Until then, it will be kept in a safe deposit box. This is a very important diary, Luci. It holds the key to your past."

Luci was determined to learn more about the Cathars and the Knights Templar and the part they played in her family's lives. She wanted to find out why the Roman Church had killed them all.

"I don't think I have told you how grateful I am to you both. You have made so many sacrifices for me."

Though they could never replace her parents, they had given her the next best thing – all their love. They had helped shape her into who she was today.

† † †

Six months later, Luci kissed her grandparents, Sarah, and Sophia goodbye. She had just gotten into her car when she heard a loud explosion that rocked her car. Turning back around, she saw her home on fire. She jumped out of her car and raced back to get her grandparents, Sarah, and Sophia out. Her next-door neighbor, Bill, grabbed her and prevented her from going in. The house was engulfed in flames within minutes. Bill sat her down on the curb and put his arm around her, trying to comfort her. She spotted Sarah racing toward her. Luci jumped up. They held onto one another and began to cry.

"What happened? Were you in the house, Sarah?"

"No, I was out in the back yard. There was a loud explosion, and I must have been knocked out. Where are Grandma and Grandpa?"

"I don't know. Maybe they're okay. Maybe they were outside, playing with Sophia. I really can't remember. Everything is fuzzy and my head hurts."

The ambulance and fire trucks arrived and tried to save Luci's home. They hooked their hoses up to the fire hydrants on the corner and blasted water in every direction at the house. The fire was out of control, the windows were exploding, and shards of glass were flying outward. Luci and Sarah could hear their grandparents' screams and tried to race back in, but the firefighters held them back. Luci couldn't breathe.

She couldn't believe that her grandparents, Gabby, and Sophia were dead. How could this happen? First her parents, and now her grandparents? Bill rushed over with a paper bag, pushed her head between her knees, and told her to breathe.

Sarah put her arms around Luci until Luci was so tired she curled into a ball and lay on the street, crying uncontrollably. Sarah stayed next to her, protecting her.

Luci felt Sarah's arms around her. Nothing seemed real. She couldn't hear the commotion going on around her and felt she was in another world. The captain of the firefighters came over and told her there were only two bodies found. They would take them to the morgue.

Luci and Sarah sat out in front of their home for hours, waiting and hoping for a miracle.

Luci got up and walked toward her home, now just a mix of ash. On the ground, she saw her teddy bear unharmed. She picked him up, then sneaked into the backyard. She heard whimpering coming from Sarah's playhouse. Sarah heard it, too. They found Sophia cowering under Sarah's computer table. Her paws were burned, but she allowed Luci to pick her up and they ran to the car with her. Luci helped Sarah get in and settled Sophia on her lap. Out of the corner of her eye, Luci spotted Gabby driving away. In her gut, Luci knew Gabby was responsible for the fire. The rage she felt toward Gabby would never be forgiven or forgotten. She tossed her bear onto the backseat and raced to the animal hospital to care for Sophia.

In every life there came a day of reckoning. Gabby would pay, Luci vowed.

The High Priestess

He (Jesus) composed a more spiritual gospel for the use of those who were perfect. It was carefully guarded, being read by those who are being initiated into the great.
~ John the Divine

Monterey State University, Monterey, California
Tuesday, 29 March, Luci aged 30
"Oh, my God, I'm late again. It's already 4:30!" Luci jumped out of bed. "Why didn't you wake me up, Louie, you silly dog?" Rubbing his head, she went on, "Let's get you outside while I change into my riding clothes."

Luci raced into the kitchen to grab a health bar out of the cabinet and a cup of already-brewed coffee, then brought her dog in and made Louie his breakfast. Sitting in the kitchen, she read the paper, drank coffee, and patted her Australian Shepherd on his head. An early riser, Luci headed off to the stables to ride her horse.

As she drove to the barn with the windows down and Adele blasting out of the radio, she began to sing "Rumors" in almost perfect harmony.

God, what a view, she thought, looking out over Highway 152 at the beautiful waterfront community and the sailboats gliding out into the bay. She noticed people unloading their kayaks off their SUVs and carrying them to the harbor. To the left, she spotted a whale-watching boat filled with tourists setting out to catch a glimpse of the California gray whales migrating to Mexico.

Slowly, she approached the tree-lined sycamore driveway of Water Falls Farm in Carmel Valley. A sign read, *Old Dogs, Young Dogs, Stupid Dogs, Drive Slowly*. Turning down the radio, she slowed her car for any dog, cat, rooster, peacock, pig, or guinea hen that might run out in front of her.

Rolling down her window, she inhaled the rich scent of hay and horses. Parking near the stalls, she smiled at the sound of the low nicker. It was her horse, Zane Gray. She got out of her car, reached into her pocket, and saw the ranch dogs running up for their daily. Walking to Zane's stall, she fed him carrots out of the carryall bag she always left in the back of her SUV. She had a bag for everything in the back. One bag held treats for all the farm animals on the property. Another bag was for her research on the Cathars. Another held her sketchpad, watercolors, and pencils so that when something attracted her attention she could stop for a while and sketch it. She really ought to get a better organizational system down. One bag could easily be mistaken for the other. What if she brought carrots to one of her lectures? she thought.

Looking up, she spotted her trainer. "Hi, Michael. Anything new?"

"Nothing, just don't stray too far off the property today. There's a coyote out on the hill, and I don't want you to be thrown off."

"Thanks. I'll stay close to the ranch."

As she was walking out the entry gates, she spotted Reynaldo. He had moved to Carmel soon after she did. She couldn't believe her old friend was still working horses.

Casually, she picked up her tack box and pulled out Gray's currycomb to brush him. Not only did this have a soothing effect on him, it also started to relax Luci for the day to come.

Gray, she thought to herself, *let's go for a walk*. Luci had a unique relationship with her horse. Sometimes it was easier to talk to him than it was to another human being. Mark Twain had said, "I have met many people in my life and that is why I love to be with dogs." He could have added horses to the list.

Saddling Gray up, she began cinching up his girth. Cinching a horse was like tying a corset on in the olden days, so she did it slowly, one hole at a time, taking a break and then cinching up another notch. She touched his sides, calming him, feeling the ripple of his muscles. Walking over to a mounting block, she climbed onto her beautiful Gray. She had always felt they made quite a pair. Him, with his dappled gray coat glimmering in the early morning sun, standing tall at sixteen-point-two hands high, and Luci, with her blonde hair, black coat, and breeches. They trotted out to the walnut trees, something her trainer told her not to do.

"Okay, Gray, we have a straight shot between the walnut groves." Luci let him go and they flew through the fields, the morning breeze catching her hair and his mane together as one. She heard the symphony of his breath, his snorts, whinnies, and his hooves as they struck the ground. The pungent scent of horse sweat and the sight of his mane whipping in the wind like a flag added to the sensory delight, bonding them. She cut across the road onto the neighboring property of Fort Ord.

† † †

Around the bend of trees, Father Del Pierro, dressed in a black leather jacket and jeans, stood watching Luci ride through the thickets. A monk in a brown habit stood silently beside him. They were waiting, watching. Del Pierro had a lot of time invested in Luci and he needed Brother John to get a good look at her for a meeting later that day.

"How did you know she would be here?" asked Tomas.

"I called Reynaldo last night; this is usually her daily routine before she heads to work."

He had contacted Janet, too. It was Luci's thirtieth birthday, and she should be receiving Esclarmonde's diary. It was important for the church and Cardinal Saachio to get the diary and its clues back to where it belonged. He had paid for a grant through church funds to get Luci inspired to find the missing treasure and the Cathar text that was most believed to have been burned by Bishop Folques. First, the monk needed to find out if Luci had received the diary.

"Why don't you just go meet up with her and tell her how proud you are of her?" asked the monk.

"Luci won't remember me. She was far too young. I may have to play another role in her life; I'll wait and see on that one. For now, it's better I stay in the shadows, helping you get the diary and her to France. There may come a day when she thinks differently about me in the end."

† † †

As Luci approached where they were, her horse shied away, as if he knew they were standing there. The horse kept backing up. Luci was worried Michael really might be right, that there was a coyote in the area. *Better be safe than sorry*, she thought.

Luci patted Gray and they trotted off back toward the barn. "It's okay, we were warned. Let's get you back home."

† † †

"Did you get a good look at her?"

"Yes, Holy Father. I will introduce myself to her in the library at the college."

"Luci is a studious woman. She's always there around seven in the morning. Speak to her right after we find the boy that her uncle Nicholas sent to deliver the diary to her for her thirtieth birthday," Del Pierro said. "Luci's friend, Jodi, lets her in the library every morning. You'll have no problems speaking to her – if all goes off as planned."

† † †

Climbing a hill, Luci stopped to rest Zane for a moment. She could see the clear blue sky overhead was a deep velvet blue, casting a soft mantle over the land. The Santa Ana winds were blowing gently down from the mountains, rustling the leaves on the trees and swaying the reeds meeting the beautiful Monterey Bay.

It was a clear day and she could see Santa Cruz. She could ride Zane forever, to get away from everyone and everything. Slowly, she picked up their trot and posted out the back side of the property where she went around the eucalyptus trees and onto the riding trail. There she stopped, watching the sun burst out of the clouds just above the mountain range.

Jumping off Zane and holding his lead rope, she let him graze while she enjoyed the quiet of the morning and the stillness of the air. Time was getting short, she thought. She needed to get Gray back.

She headed back to the barn, hitched her horse to a post, and began to pull off his tack gently. She curried him and gave him a quick scratch under his chin. Taking the lead rope, she led him back into his stall.

Before leaving the barn, she gave Zane a peppermint and watched as he enjoyed his treat. He always gave her hope – the hope of making her dreams a reality. She never felt lonely when she was with Zane. Slowly, walking back to her SUV, she waved to Dawn, the owner of the stable.

"How's your class going?" Dawn called out.

"Okay. I'm teaching the mysteries of the Bible this semester, its textual criticism, trying to reconstruct the author's original intent based on variant copies of manuscripts. I want to put a little history behind it and put it into context regarding the Cathars and the Albignesian wars."

Dawn said, "Oh, I almost forgot, there was a lady looking for you yesterday."

"What did she want?"

"Something about you going to France. Don't know for sure, I really wasn't listening. She just said she worked with you. She had black hair, pulled back in a tight bun."

"She's the dean of my department. France? I don't think so."

"Seemed like a bitch. She yelled at Reynaldo," she said, walking away.

She is, Luci thought.

Puzzled at the thought of Janet being at the ranch and speaking to Reynaldo, Luci figured she'd better see what was up. She usually avoided Janet at all cost.

She got into her SUV and headed down highway 156 toward the university, hoping to hit the school library before class. Entering the campus, she slipped into a parking space, barely beating out a student for those coveted spots in Lot A, just a few feet from her class. She exited the car and walked past the campus living quarters toward the library.

Opening the door, she saw her friend, Jodi, working behind the research counter.

"Do you want the same book, *The Song of the Cathars*?"

"Yes, please. The guy who wrote it, Bishop Folques, was mean, but, according to Professor Janet Gaetos, 'the Little Keys of Solomon' are in it."

"What are those?"

"There is a tradition that suggests that those who possess the secret writing known as 'the Little Keys of Solomon' possess the understanding and knowledge of where the lost temple of Solomon can be found and its treasures."

"So what does he have to do with all of this?" Jodi asked.

"Think about it. Isn't it likely that one of the Cathars gave out the secret? Folques never found it, but these keys include the application of numerology, astrology, and the tarot cards. So in writing this, he might have been trying to figure them out."

"Sounds like a guy I dated last week." Jodi added, "How about lunch after my class this afternoon?"

"Great. One o'clock?"

"We can meet at the FishWife. They serve an incredible bowl of clam chowder and have a mean hot sauce. Oh, before I forget, one of the janitors spotted a grungy-looking guy in the bathroom. It's probably nothing. Just be careful."

"Thanks. I'll keep an eye out for anything spooky," Luci smiled.

† † †

After climbing up the stairs to the lounge, Luci wandered over to a secluded area where she found a quiet place with a soft chair to nestle into for a few hours without disturbance, and began reading up on the Cathars for the day's lecture. Jotting down notes, she didn't get very far in her research when a young man approached her from behind. He was wearing what she thought were dirty jeans and a black hoodie that concealed his face. She angled her body away from him and turned her chair. At this time of the morning, very few people were on campus, let alone in the library.

Leaning close to her, he whispered, "Take this book."

Turning swiftly at the intrusion, she fell out of her seat and got her legs tangled up in the chair, yelling from the ground, "Holy shit!"

"Luci, shut up. I don't have time," he said as he grabbed her arm. "Take this. It will lead you to the keys. It belongs to your family. Nicholas entrusted this to me to give to you. I've got to get out of here before someone sees me with you."

"Nick?"

"Your uncle, Luci."

"Wait, you know my uncle?"

"Yes, now shhh." He was crying.

"It's going to be okay," she told him. Trying to calm the shaking man down, she slowly stood up and sat back in her chair. "You're safe here. No one is going to hurt you," she said, placing her hand on his shoulder.

As she was quietly talking to him, she held her phone under the library table and punched 8011 for the university police. He was young and with wisps of hair on his chin. *It's funny the things you notice.*

Pulling her hand off his knee, she looked down. It was sticky with blood. She gasped, but the boy covered her mouth with his hand. She looked into his eyes and saw fear.

Pulling his hand away from her mouth she said, "You need a doctor. Let me call an ambulance," pulling her phone off her lap.

"I don't have much time. Just take the book," he said as he shoved it into her hands.

Luci saw that his right hand was also covered in blood. His jeans were bloody, not dirty. "My God, let me help you."

"He's close. I've got to get away. Be careful, Luci," he said as tears fell down his face.

Luci was bewildered and frightened. This was just too much. She looked around, but there was no one she could turn to for help.

"The longer I stay, the more danger I put you in," he said.

"Please don't go. An ambulance is on its way. Let me help you. I don't want you to die. Please don't die. You know about my family. Please, just wait a few minutes. The ambulance will be here. What's your name?" She looked down and saw that it had writing on it in the Occitan language.

She raised her eyes and the young man was gone. Immediately, she redialed the campus police operator and described the youth as best as she could. "Please, he needs help. He's bleeding badly. You've got to find him," she begged, hoping for quick action.

The police commanded her to stay where she was and told her they would look for him and then come get her.

Conflicted about leaving, she tried opening the package. Her hands were shaking. She pulled out an old leather-bound book. She had seen this book once before – on her eighteenth birthday. It was Esclarmonde's diary.

Terrified, she opened the book, just a crack, not wanting to damage its ancient spine. Inside, she discovered a tarot card, the Moon. She remembered little about the tarot from when Sister Catherine taught her when she'd been a child, but it had been so long ago. She was aware that each one stood for something, but she wasn't sure anymore what it meant. She began to read the diary's first entry.

Esclarmonde's Diary

March, 1204

I kneeled and watched from behind a high hill where the crusader and I hid, as a detachment of knights led Almaric and Folques through the carnage-strewn city toward the church of St Mary Magdalene, where the last of the Occitan survivors had barricaded themselves. I heard later what Folques and Almaric said to each other.

Folques asked why they had not taken the church. The knight replied that the beams were far too strong. Folques yelled at him and said they would starve them out.

I watched as Almaric looked at the thick oak planks that framed the church's bell tower. "Do you have a man who can send a flaming arrow on top of the roof?"

The knight turned to look at the abbot in disbelief. "There are ten thousand people crammed inside the church, most loyal Catholics," the knight said.

"I'm not staying here all summer. An example needs to be made."

"What about our own believers?" questioned the knight. "There are more of them inside the church than Cathars."

In horror, I watched as Almaric meditated on the jeweled crucifix at his breast. After a moment of prayer, he made the sign of the cross on the church doors as if dispensing the sacrament of penance. He turned to his knight and ordered, "Kill them all."

The knights traded startled glances. "But there are innocents among them," the knight replied.

"God will know his own. Now light the arrow."

The Moon

And (remember) when God proclaimed:
If you are grateful I will give you more; but if you are ungrateful,
verily my punishment is indeed severe.
~ The Koran

Luci aged 30
Luci raced down the stairwell and got on a computer, quickly looking for the Moon in the Visconti-Sforza deck in the tarot.

Jodi walked up behind her. "Why are you looking up something on the tarot?"

"It has to do with the boy you saw, the one the janitor told you about. He was drenched in his own blood. The poor kid, he was wandering around the campus looking for me."

"Did you call campus police?"

"Of course. They are out on campus looking for him."

"What does the tarot card say?"

"It states, hidden enemies."

"What's that supposed to mean?"

"I guess it means that the boy had an enemy and should have taken more precautions."

"But it was given to you, Luci." Looking over Luci's shoulder, Jodi pointed to the next sentence. "It also means danger, darkness, terror, and deception."

This doesn't sound very good, Luci thought, beginning to panic. "I've got to get out of here."

†††

Luci knew the tarot cards had their beginning early in history. She pulled the diary out of her backpack. It didn't look any different from any other book in the library – old and musty. However, written by her relative, Esclarmonde, it was a first-hand account of

the Cathars and the part the Knights Templar played in the Albignesian war.

"How did that kid know my uncle and how did he get hold of my
family's diary? And where in the hell are the police?" she muttered,
her mind searching for answers.

Getting up, she began to move toward the library entrance when
she spotted her boss, Janet. Luci walked down the stairs to the
main section of the library to speak to the dean about France and
why she'd yelled at Reynaldo.

"Luci, we need to have a word in my office," Janet said, beating
her to the punch.

"I'll be right there. I was told to wait for the police. They're
arriving any minute and told me to stay put."

"You just checked out a book that I want. Please hand it over."

"I need this information for my class in ancient archaeology, Dr
Gaetos."

"No need to stand on formalities. You do remember me, don't
you?" Dr Gaetos asked.

"You mean from the orphanage? I've always known, but have
chosen to forget that time in my life and the bullies who picked on
Sarah and me. I have a happy life and I won't let anyone in who
wants to destroy my happiness. And you, Janet, could destroy
that."

"So you do remember."

"Like I said, it was a long time ago."

"I just don't want you to forget who's in charge. So when I say
hand over the book, that is exactly what I mean."

"Still a bully, I see," Luci responded. Reaching into her backpack, with her sweater covering the diary, she handed Janet Gaetos *The Song of the Cathars*.

† † †

Janet leaned over, hoping to get a look at anything else hidden in
Luci's backpack. Father Del Pierro had said Luci should be receiving it today, but all she saw was a sweater. *I guess the monk will have
to have a word with Luci*, Janet thought. Seizing *The Song of the
Cathars*, she turned and walked out the library door.

† † †

She tried to settle herself down after her encounter with her boss by sinking deep into a cushy chair. Luci pulled out Esclarmonde's diary from her bag.

"Can I have a word with you, Luci?" A man in a brown robe appeared out of nowhere.

Looking closely, she noticed he was a monk. He was short and stout, with narrow features and a bowl cut that looked like it came right out of the Middle Ages. Their eyes met. His were as dark as death. She didn't know how he knew her name, but she needed air. He pulled a tarot card out of the pocket in his robe and placed it on the table in front of her. He had blood on his hands.

Intrigued by the card, but not wanting to make a scene, she said, "Sorry, I have to go teach my class and I'm late. Can we get together later today?"

"Luci, I have been waiting to speak with you," the monk said anxiously. "A young man gave you something that belongs to the church. Please hand it over."

This was the guy who hurt the kid. "Sorry, I don't know what you're talking about," she said hastily.

She was feeling trapped and afraid. It was now about eight-thirty in the morning. There were students coming onto campus for their classes. They stopped what they were doing as the monk lunged for Lucy, grabbing her arm.

"Are you okay, Ms de Foix?" asked one of Luci's students.

"If you say anything to this student, you'll be responsible for his death, do you understand?" he whispered.

"It's okay, Kevin. He's a friend. Go over to the Religion aisle. We will be having a discussion on the Albigensian Wars."

"Are you sure?" Kevin said hesitantly.

Smiling, she said, "Yes, thank you, Kevin. You don't have long before class, so get to it."

"Okay," he said, smiling back at her and leaving.

"Now, that's a good girl, Luci. We're going to get along just fine. I just need you to come with me."

His nails dug into her arm. He smelled of dirt, and she wanted no part in going anywhere with him. Luci pulled her arm away and began walking quickly down the stairs and out the library door. She broke into a run, past the picnic tables, toward her classroom. The monk was closing in on her. She pushed the table down behind her and began to run faster. The monk stumbled over the table. Luci saw Janet race toward the monk. Luci tried to warn her away, but she saw that Janet couldn't hear her above the screams of sirens and kids scrambling trying to get out of the way of the monk who was now brandishing a knife. The monk began to move toward Luci, circling a water fountain in the middle of the quad, when he collided with a police officer who had just gotten out of his car.

The police officer shoved the monk into the fountain's brick wall, which caused him to drop the knife.

Luci noticed immediately that the assailant was covering up a very muscular body. He seemed angry and afraid of the attack by the young police officer. The monk rolled over and kneed the cop in the groin. The breath left the officer in a loud gasp, and Luci could see he was in agony. Then the monk sprang to his feet, glared at her, and ran off past the library.

More police cars finally began to appear. One screeched to a stop near Willet Hall. Another came up on Diversity Street surrounding the quad. The monk was cornered inside the plaza near Tortuga Hall. He hesitated for just a moment, then maneuvered around the construction material surrounding the Visitors' Center, where he raced up the stairs. What was he doing? There was no way out besides the front entrance.

The cops raced through the building, throwing open the doors to every room.

Looking up, Luci spotted the monk standing on the third-floor balcony of the center. He seemed frightened. He turned and looked behind him as if he was listening to someone. Then he faced back toward the railing, made the sign of the cross, and pitched himself forward.

"No!" Luci couldn't stop screaming.

He landed, arms outstretched, on some metal spikes jutting out of the concrete slab. Luci saw he was still holding the tarot card. It was the card of Justice.

She tore herself away from the horrible sight and scanned the crowd searching for Janet. She couldn't see her anywhere. The ambulance and fire truck were arriving.

Too many people, too much noise, Luci could barely breathe. She saw Janet walking out of the Visitors' Center. Luci grabbed a sack of birdseed she always carried to feed the birds on her break. Dumping the seeds out she began to breathe into the paper bag. How could the monk have known about the book, and why had he wanted it enough to die? Her skin went clammy as she fought for breath.

The paramedics raced over to the monk and immediately pronounced him dead. Someone pointed Luci out to the second paramedic. He raced over to her, then slipped an oxygen mask over her nose.

"Breathe," he said.

She could hear people off in the distance. Someone said, "I think she's having a heart attack."

Hearing that, Luci grabbed the oxygen mask out of the EMT's hand and sucked the oxygen out even harder while holding her backpack close to her chest. She wasn't letting go. Still, she began to lose consciousness.

"Don't go to sleep," the paramedic said. "Stay with me and keep breathing."

The last thing she heard before the ambulance door closed was Janet's harsh whisper near her ear. "Don't think you're getting out of going to France, Luci."

† † †

The detective watched as the monk's body was pulled off the metal spikes and laid it on the street beneath a yellow tarp. The police were busy moving curious students away from the scene. Edging through the crowd, Janet watched as the police pulled the tarp away and the photographer began taking pictures. The monk's arm was contorted in an unnatural position, his skull caved in, his torso crushed, and his legs twisted, as if he had no bones.

"Don't leave," the police captain told Janet. "Did you know the deceased?"

"No. I was coming to see a colleague who was in the library and then I saw her run out with the monk chasing her."

"Don't go far. We need a statement from you." Looking over his shoulder, he called out to an officer. "Follow the ambulance to the hospital and see if you can get a statement from the woman who just left. What's her name?"

"Dr Luci de Foix," Gaetos said to the officer.

She did not intend to leave the scene, dead monk or not. She had been waiting for years for Esclarmonde's diary to surface, and she was sure Luci now had it in her possession.

Father Del Pierro stood, looking out at the mess he'd paid that nut Janet to prevent. This was the same messed up girl he had known very intimately at the orphanage. He should have killed her when he had the opportunity.

† † †

Luci stayed the night at the hospital where they gave her Clonazepam and Ativan. Slowly, she began to recover.

The doctor said she'd had a panic attack, not a heart attack. Nothing to worry about, though. She knew she'd had one before at the Monterey horse show, but her grandmother had given her a bag to breathe into and she'd been fine.

Now her thoughts were tangled up inside her head. It wasn't the first time she'd witnessed someone dying, but it was still horrific. She could hear the sound of the monk's body when it slammed into the pavement with a sickening thud.

Sensations of panic again coursed through her as she began to think about the accident she had been in as a child, along with today's sirens, the dead monk, and the reason she had run out of the library. She needed to move out of this hospital and to her home in Pacific Grove. The doctors said they would release her in the afternoon. She climbed out of the bed and grabbed her backpack from the closet where she'd seen the nurse put it. She put it under her pillow for safekeeping. She wasn't sure what was going on, but she felt it had something to do with the diary. Her mind was racing. *Where was Janet?*

Why is this happening to me?

The Devil

*A small body of determined spirits fired by an unquenchable faith
in their mission can alter the course of history.*
~ Mohandas Gandhi

Father Nathaniel Del Pierro approached the secluded household among the sycamore trees in Monterey. The sidewalk in front of Janet's home was deserted. His physical description was surely on file from witnesses in the student-welcoming center at the college by now. Therefore, he stored his Roman collar and was dressed in jeans and a black leather jacket. He knew Janet had late-night visitors, so another man would go unnoticed. However, it was important that he linger no longer than necessary.

He had brought the monk with him from the Vatican and they had planned every detail of their action, along with Cardinal Saachio, a member of the Vatican Council and Treasurer of Banco Ambrosia. The Vatican was in chaos because two factions held sway. The Machiavellian maneuvering and incessant power struggle were very much like years gone by. He sided with Cardinal Vito Saachio, an administrator in line for succession if the Pope died. Saachio also held two tarot cards, the Devil and the Star. According to tarot, the Devil was the opposite of the Lovers' card. The Romans believed the Cathars were the Devil incarnate.

They believed there were four great Devils, according to Prefect Belibaste: the Pope, the King of France, the Bishop of Parmiers, the Lord Inquisitor of Carcassonne, and a fifth was predicted to come in the future. They had been searching for the family who held Esclarmonde's diary for years. It was believed to contain the whereabouts of the "The Little Keys of Solomon" that confided who the fifth "Devil" would be and where the treasure was. They were getting close to retrieving it. His confidant, Reynaldo, had never let him down.

"Good." He could see Janet's car parked in the driveway. He and Janet needed to have a little chat.

†††

Janet grabbed a wine bottle from her cabinet and walked to her desk. She had meticulously searched through the university's library for papers written by Pope Innocent III. She wondered if Luci remembered her from the orphanage and had been one of Father Del Pierro's playthings, as she had once been. It didn't really matter now, it was in the past.

She wanted the diary for herself. Luci was just a pawn, and, one day, Janet would kill her. Janet would never forget how Luci had humiliated her in front of the girls at the orphanage, and she would have to pay for it.

The diary held clues that would lead to the lost treasure, hidden by Esclarmonde and her brother, Loup. Luci, the ungrateful bitch, was more of a problem than Janet could tolerate. This needed to end, but just not yet. She still required Luci.

Picking up her phone, she dialed the stables. "Reynaldo, keep an eye on Luci and let me know if she goes out to the barn."

"I will, Dr Gaetos," he said. "What else do you need for me to do today?"

"Come by my house this evening and just check around. See if you notice anything out of the ordinary. I had to suggest to the monk today that he should jump off a balcony. The police were closing in on him. I let him know what American men do to pedophiles in prison. We need to get that diary and find out who else is interested in finding the treasure of Solomon."

"The monk was a friend of Father Del Pierro. He will be angry with you."

"If he had been caught, it would have been worse for all of us," Janet said.

"I'll put the blankets on the horses and drop by later," he said, hanging up the phone.

Father Del Pierro had taught her how to survive, but she would never forget the day he'd called her into his room. Taking another sip of her wine, she thought back on the day. She'd been a frightened young student with no friends, who'd been abandoned by her parents to the church. Del Pierro had sucked her in, plied her with treats, told her how beautiful she was, and then, one day, when he called her into his room, he'd locked the door. He'd told her she had been naughty and to pull her dress up and her panties down. Frightened, she obeyed. He'd told her to turn around. She did as she was told. All of a sudden, she could feel his cold hands grasp her buttocks. He was so close she could feel his warm breath on her neck.

"Don't say a word and never tell anyone."

She would never forget that message as he'd plunged deep inside her anus while holding her mouth shut. She tried to tear away from his grip, silently screaming.

He'd zipped up his pants and looked at her with disdain. "Leave."

That was all he said.

She'd left his office, broken, bleeding, and humiliated.

It's time I break away from this devil. The monk told her before he died that he saw the diary in Luci's backpack. *Now that she knew Luci had the information, she would make sure she got on that plane to France.* She'd go if she wanted tenure. With Luci's help, she'd get that treasure.

† † †

Father Del Pierro tripped the front door lock and entered the home. He crept past the kitchen to the rear of the cluttered ground floor. No sound betrayed his presence. Silently, he stepped through an open doorway into a lighted den. Dr Janet Gaetos was stretched out on her reading chair, a glass of red wine in her hand, which had spilled over her 1970's dressing gown. A large cross hung around her neck and another uncorked bottle of wine sat on the table beside her.

He caught a look of disbelief on her face that she quickly masked. "Come in, Father. I'm boiling some water on the stove. Would you care for a cup of tea?" she asked while getting up from her chair. "What are you doing here?"

"We had an arrangement," he said as he leaned against the wall. "I give you five million dollars to tell Luci it's a grant from a benefactor for her continued research into the lost documents and treasures of the Cathars. That should get her attention."

"I will," Janet exclaimed. "I can't help it that the monk screwed things up by knifing the kid. He was just supposed to come over to talk to Luci and me, and then I could introduce her to him. What was I supposed to do?"

"You said there would be no problems with Luci. That she trusted you." He moved closer to the door.

"She doesn't trust me; she does what I tell her to do," Janet said. "She was afraid of the monk. Hell, *I* was afraid of him."

"You seem to be playing both sides, Janet. Saachio wants that diary. I have people watching everywhere, so don't think you can get away with it or the treasure. You're not that smart."

Everything was happening a little too fast for Janet to think in her wine-induced state. She needed more time.

† † †

Del Pierro wondered if Janet thought him that stupid. "Don't make us regret our decision after all these years. You *can* be replaced."

"After all of these years, who could replace me?" she asked, slurring her words.

Ignoring her sarcasm, Del Pierro continued, "Luci needs to be on a plane to France. Now she has the diary with the codes, she has the key. We need to stop the Cathars before Luci finds the lost codex of the Cathars and the treasure."

"What lost codex? I only know about the treasure. How in the hell do you know she is that important, for God's sake?"

"I would be very cautious in the way you speak to me, Janet," he scolded.

Feeling chastised by the priest, she asked, "Why is this diary so important that I have spent my life babysitting Luci de Foix?"

"It is important to the church, which is all that you need to know. Saachio has been instrumental in putting the next Italian pope in place. He has packed the curia with Italian friends of influential means. This diary could lead to the codex that, one day, could destroy the church that Peter built."

"And the treasure?"

"It could fill the Banco de Ambrosia."

"Haven't I always done what you and Cardinal Saachio wanted? You'll gain influence over the election of the next pope should Pope Paul meet a premature death," Janet said. She knew she was playing a dangerous game now; he couldn't know how much she hated him.

"This will bring back Italy after two successive non-Italian popes who broke what has been an Italian monopoly for over four hundred and fifty years. Remember, seven of the eighteen new cardinal electors are Italian. Six of them work for Saachio in the curia. We have a lot at stake. The codex must not be made public," Del Pierro reminded her.

"I checked on her at the Monterey Peninsula hospital. She doesn't suspect me of anything," Janet reported.

The small room reeked of alcohol. Hundreds of books lay scattered among stacks of newspapers and magazines. He wondered how she could live like this. "She better not, bitch."

Janet threw her glass of wine at him. She had flashbacks of him raping her as a young child. "How dare you?"

Slowly, he wiped off the red wine that was dripping down the front of his jacket and calmly said, "How dare I what?"

She wasn't about to bring up the past. Instead, she said, "Since Luci believes I am her mentor, I can go over to her home and ask her if she has ever heard of Esclarmonde. We can discuss what she wants to do with her academic career, life, the Cathars, and the Knights Templar … just a friendly chit-chat between colleagues. Maybe she will show me the book. If so, I'll watch where she puts it. Later, I can have Reynaldo steal it," she offered. Over many discussions through the course of years in which Luci worked for Janet, she knew that Luci had been told very little about her heritage and probably had no clue of her importance.

Del Pierro already knew what course of action he was about to take. He'd gotten tired of this spray-tanned alcoholic. "Actually, why do we need you?"

"All I'm asking for is a little more time. You'll have the book, Father Del Pierro," she said.

He slammed a fist into her gut. Janet doubled over and then slumped forward, held upright by his arm.

"I wanted the monk to have a talk with Luci. We paid you handsomely to get her in a secluded place where the monk could get the information from her in a very quiet way. You killed my friend. You were once useful, Janet, but that's no longer the case."

"I – can get the – book," Janet stuttered between halted breaths. Turning, she picked up a letter opener that was sitting on the table.

"You're wrong. In fact, I think I can get the book from Luci. Unlike you, she is pretty. You've become a wreck. Your skin is sagging and yellow." He looked at her with disgust. "The church will thank me, and I'll get something good in the bargain."

"Hello, Reynaldo. Glad you could make it," Janet addressed someone suddenly standing behind Del Pierro. She smiled so wide that, when her lips parted, they looked like a red apple splitting open.

"You don't expect me to turn and look, while you grab for that letter opener, do you, Janet?"

"Actually, I don't need to. Good night, Father." Janet turned to walk out of the room and felt something sting her right arm. Ducking around the kitchen door, she ran out and down the street. She turned and looked at her arm in disbelief. Reynaldo had shot her. He had betrayed her for Del Pierro. My God, she had trusted him all these years. He'd been in bed with Del Pierro all this time. Bastard. *He'll die for this*, she vowed, grabbing her arm.

The Emperor

But there was a man named Simon, who had previously practised magic in the city and amazed the nation of Samaria, saying that he, himself was somebody great, to whom they all gave heed, from the least to the greatest, saying, "This man has the power of God, for a long time he had bewitched them with sorceries."
~ Acts 8:9-11

After a night's stay at the hospital and plenty of rest, Luci headed for home in Pacific Grove. Approaching her complex, she could hear the shrieking and twittering of the starlings, wrens, and linnets on the trees above her. She approached her driveway slowly so the deer that lived around her home in the Del Monte forest would not run into the street and get hurt. The sun was just rising and she could smell the ocean air. Parking her car in the garage, she entered her home through the garage door, flipping on the lights, and dropping her backpack onto the kitchen table. She spotted the Emperor, another tarot card, on the table. She began to tremble and ran into her bedroom to fetch her old teddy bear. She found a brown paper bag and started breathing deeply, slowing herself down.

She reached for the phone and dialed 911 to report the break-in.

"Do you know if someone is in your home now?"

"I don't know," she said, fingering the little hole that was now getting larger on her bear.

"We'll send a patrol car over to check inside and out."

While Luci was walking toward the bedroom door, Louie, the Australian Shepherd, came running out of the back bedroom and ran over, licking her hand, trying to comfort in the only way he knew.

After her grandparents had died in the fire, she began volunteering at the Animal Friends Shelter for Dogs and Cats. One day, an Australian Shepherd arrived from Fresno. He looked so much like her old dog, Sophia, who had died long ago. He was a blue merle, with one ice blue eye and the other, brown. Luci picked him up and he cuddled up on her shoulder and neck. She immediately filled out an application, and, within days he was hers. Luci named him Louie after her grandfather.

When Luci felt calmer, she and Louie walked around the condominium with a baseball bat she had hidden in her front closet. They went from room to room, but since there were very few rooms there wasn't a lot hidden from view.

While waiting for the police to arrive, Luci opened her laptop and looked up the Emperor from the tarot deck of Marseilles. She knew that, unknown to most people, the tarot was initially meant to be like baseball cards. The Emperor was defined as materialistic. He faced sideways, which translated to being removed from power. On his shield was a Phoenix, a messenger from heaven or a politically loyal person. Finding nothing lurking behind the cabinets, closets, or under the bed, Luci closed her laptop and walked into the kitchen to feed Louie.

Then she picked up the diary. Opening it carefully, she read Esclarmonde's account of The Knights Templar. In it, Esclarmonde wrote that in one of their battles the knights overtook a town in the Middle East and murdered all the people.

I wonder why they did this, weren't they supposed to be the good guys of that time?

Esclarmonde's Diary

May, 1204

I hid behind a secret wall in the church rectory and a knight grabbed my friend, the curator of the library.

"We have heard of an ancient manuscript given to Mary of Magdala from Jesus about a treasure. Tell me where it is."

I could see my friend was terrified. He looked over to where I was and warned me to stay silent. He would never give up the sacred scrolls even if forced to.

The knight pulled out his knife and plucked out the curator's eye. Screaming and crying, the librarian, when questioned, continued to deny knowledge of the artefact. The knights formed a ring around the librarian.

I covered my mouth to protect myself from discovery. It was only a matter of time before they tortured him so much he would have no choice but to tell.

"Please," I heard him beg, "I have made a pledge to protect the library. I don't know what you want." He watched as some of the young knights burned all of the sacred documents that'd been written over many years. "We are a poor village. We have nothing. Just leave us, please." He was in agony and crying as he held his hand over his bloody, empty eye socket.

The knight took the bloody knife, grabbed the old man, and plucked out the other eye without uttering a word.

The old man fell to his knees, bleeding profusely. The knights looked on without compassion. They listened to the librarian as he screamed in pain and begged for mercy.

The knight screamed at him, "Your books are for heretics and all who read them should burn! We came for the scroll taken by John, the disciple of Jesus. We are going to find your wife, your children, and your grandchildren, and I will take their eyes out, one by one, unless you tell me where the scroll is. Now give me what I have asked for."

I made a dash to where the sacred scrolls were placed for centuries. Grabbing them, I left the library and ran to warn the curator's family to leave. I watched as they packed what little belongings they had left in their home and placed them in the wagon. I jumped on my white steed and raced to Montsegur.

Temperance

Are you able to drink from the cup that I drink, or to be baptized with the baptism with which I was baptized?
~ Mark 10:38

Luci aged 30
Picking up Louie's bowl from the kitchen floor, Luci poured kibble in it and continued to read Esclarmonde's diary. Jesus had told Mary Magdalene about angels who would help people transition into heaven. When the Knights Templar read about the scroll, they began to understand its significance. They were extremely excited to share their knowledge.

Yes, Luci thought, *but I bet they realized that if they took this information back to the pope, he would declare them heretics due to the rigidity of the Roman Church.*

Luci knew very little about Mary Magdalene, but found information on the web regarding the 1945 scrolls discovered by two goat herders in Egypt. Luci called up her sister Sarah, who was now the executive vice president of a computer company. She had changed from the meek, mousy-haired girl from the orphanage, to a strong, vibrant, intelligent woman. "Sarah, have you ever heard of the Nag Hammadi Scrolls?"

"Sure. I saw something about it on the History Channel a couple of years ago. They're documents written by Jesus's brother James, a disciple named Thomas, John the Divine, and Mary Magdalene. They hold important information about a treasure they had secreted away."

"Yeah, but this discovery, although important, had been deemed unimportant at the time to the papacy. Why? It wasn't even included with the main texts of Mathew, Mark, Luke, and John in the Bible. You don't even hear it mentioned by the Catholic Church today."

Luci lifted the diary that had enchanted her as when she first saw it. It had beautiful pictures imprinted in gold. Originally, there had been no book jacket protecting the cloth-bound cover. At one time, it looked like it had been a deep burgundy, but it was now faded to a light violet. The pages were tissue-thin, gilt-edged, and littered with engravings. The title was still visible in patchy gold lettering.

"It's a diary that gives an account of the tragic events that led to the end of the Cathars, the Knights Templar, and quite possibly leads to a codex hidden by the Cathars for safekeeping."

"What is Esclarmonde's importance to the Nag Hammadi?"

"It's not so much her importance, but that of her Aunt Corba. She became an important Cathar Prefect and received the consolamentum and, with that honor, she came into control of many important documents. She was an heir to Montsegur and she built schools and hostels to shelter Cathars who were in danger. She was also responsible for its refortification."

"I'll look her up to see what I can find out about her," Sarah said

"That'd be great, Sarah."

"Corba lived in a town called Laurac. It was the home of the Cathar Bishop of Toulouse and has been described by the church as the 'seat of Satan and capital of heresy' by those who conquered it. Corbas's only son, Aimeri de Montreal, died in the battle of Lavaur along with four hundred Cathars who were burned at the stake. After the battle, eighty knights hung from the castle wall as a warning. Corba's daughter was thrown down a well and covered with rocks," Sarah reported to Luci.

"Isn't she the Prefect who chose to end her life by jumping off the castle tower instead of submitting to the pope's knights? I remember a legend that some people still believe she never hit the ground but turned into a dove and soared away," said Luci.

"Isn't there a window at the Cathedral of Notre Dame de Chartres in honor of a Cathar woman?" asked Sarah

"You know I've never been to France. Is there?" Luci responded.

"Yes, there is."

"A little. I don't seem to be able to get over the fear of large crowds and flying on planes. But this would be a really good reason for me to try to figure out a way," Luci confided.

"Actually, I think it would. I heard somewhere that life is a race between indifference and danger and that it comes down to confidence in ourselves. I think if you put together the clues between the Cathars, the tarot will help you to find that confidence in yourself and help you find who killed your parents."

"This is important, I know. The Temperance card in Esclarmonde's diary talks about things being connected with the church and with a religious sect. It's a place between death and the devil."

"I have my old travel guide from when I visited. Let me look up St Chartres Cathedral. It says in this guide that when it was built, women had no place in the cathedral. Only later did statues and stained glass windows with women become introduced," Sarah read.

"Could the lady in the Rose Window be Corba?" Luci asked.

"Most people believe that it was the Knights Templar who finished building the cathedral, so I tend to believe that it's possible it was Mary Magdalene with Mary, Jesus's mother, and another young girl named Mary who traveled with Joseph of Aramethea. She was on a boat to the shores of France, carrying something important after the death of Jesus. Some say it was Peter, the disciple, who pushed the three out onto the water rudderless."

"How sad – the jealousy that Peter had for Mary Magdalene," Sarah said as an afterthought.

"It could also be Corba de Foix pictured in the window."

"I *would* really like to see it one day."

"Luci, what better time than now, especially that it's paid for?"

"I've heard of the beautiful towers in Languedoc, the churches devoted to Mary, and maybe there is some clue in the window. Esclarmonde describes herself as having the green eyes of her ancestors, and she was a warrior. She fought the Teutonic knights alongside her brother, Loup."

While speaking with Luci, Sarah began flipping the channels on the TV, "Hey, are you watching the news?" Sarah chimed in.

Carrying the book to her recliner, Luci turned on the TV and settled into the cushions. Turning on the six o'clock news, she saw where the monk had died. Something tugged at the back of her mind, something about the monk dying the way he did.

"Weren't you there yesterday when the monk died?" Sarah asked.

"Yes, shush, I can't hear. What's the newsman saying?"

"Did you see it happen?"

"I was there and saw him land on spikes." She didn't want to tell Sarah that she'd had a panic attack. She felt like such a wimp. She could handle nunchucks, coin swords, axes, and had taken down several opponents in mock fights at the studio and at tournaments across the country. "It was horrible," Luci continued. "He tried to talk to me just before he jumped, but I was afraid of him."

"Is that why you ended up in the hospital? God, I hope they gave you enough drugs."

"Enough to make me believe that I can leave Montercy and find out more about the tarot deck of cards and Esclarmonde's diary."

"Are you sure you're *up* to this?" Sarah asked, incredulously.

"I don't think I have a choice, but I need you to babysit Louie for me."

"Of course I will, and, remember, I'm only a phone call or computer click away."

The Magician

If you take any activity, any art, any discipline, any skill –
take it and push it as far as it will go, push it beyond where it has ever
been before, push it to the wildest edges of the edges, then you force it into
the realm of magic.
~ Tom Robbins

Max Dantie arrived too late at the Monterey Bay Hospital to question Luci de Foix, a witness to the death of a Catholic monk. After showing credentials and a friendly smile, he was able to get Luci's address from the attending nurse. He needed to follow up on what the professor might know of the incident, but uppermost

in his mind was why the monk tried to accost her. He didn't think
the monk would be so bold without reason.

Max had checked out the video surveillance in San Francisco
airport. He was more concerned with Father Del Pierro, the man
who had picked up the monk and what this had to do with Luci.
He knew this was just the beginning of his journey.

The following evening, he walked up the driveway lined by
eucalyptus trees and saw the front porch light on. He rang the
doorbell and waited for someone to answer. Inside, he could hear
a dog barking.

The door slowly opened, just enough to prevent a large Australian Shepherd from jumping on him.

"Dr de Foix? My name is Officer Dantie. I'd like to ask you
about your report of a burglary and what happened at the college
today."

"May I see some identification?"

"Sure. Does he bite?" he asked, looking down at the dog.

"Louie? Only if told to," she said with a slight grin, holding out
her hand.

The officer handed his badge over to Luci for inspection.

She noticed he was wearing a very unusual ring. It looked like a
double Star of David, but with an amethyst in the middle. She held
his badge under the light for a closer look and memorized his
badge number.

Louie snared. "Louie, get back," she commanded.

† † †

She noticed he seemed to have drifted off. "Officer Dantie, sir,
how can I help you?"

He cleared his throat. "Sorry to bother you," he said, looking
down at his watch. "I know it's late, but I have a few questions to
ask you regarding the incident that happened yesterday afternoon.
You also reported a robbery today. What have you noticed missing?"

"Actually, I reported someone in my home and it isn't what they
stole, but what they left."

"What would that be, Ms de Foix?"

"They left a tarot card."

He smiled. "I'll make a note of that. Is there anything else?"

"Just the fact that someone was in my home after I witnessed a monk taking a header off a balcony and landing on construction spikes."

"I'd like to ask you about that. Do you have any idea why he did that?"

"I have no idea. It's all too overwhelming for me."

She shoved the stray hair from her face and as she did she became aware of the officer staring at her. He briefly touched her handing over his identification when her hair on her arms began to rise and her skin heated up. The officer had dark wavy hair, and liquid dark eyes. She was instantly attracted, which was bizarre under the circumstance.

"Come in, Officer. I was wondering the same thing," she said as she led him into her front room.

Walking in, she watched as he gazed around the neat but straightforward furnishings in her home. There were books of every description lined up neatly on bookshelves, with a few open on an old glass mahogany table. She appeared to have been sitting in the chair before he came to the door. Louie was curled up on the sofa, watching him intently, and didn't look like he was about to share his seat. He stood perplexed looking at the dog.

She felt the officer's discomfort and said, "Wait a second. I'll get a chair for you. Won't take me but a minute. It's just in the kitchen. Louie doesn't like to share his favorite section of the sofa, and, honestly, you would be covered in hair. Sit here," she said, lugging the heavy chair into the front room."

"Let me help you."

"It's okay. I have horses so I'm used to pushing and pulling things around. How can I help you?"

Luci recognized he was the same officer at the crime scene who had been watching her. She watched as he looked her up and down. She knew she should have been wearing a bra and moved her arms up covering the silhouette of her breasts against her T-shirt from the chill and dampness in the air. "I left Dr Gaetos' home not long ago and she suggested that I speak with you. She didn't have any idea why you thought you were being chased. She did say you were doing research in the library on the Cathars, is that right?"

"Yes, I was doing it for my class I was to teach later that afternoon. I don't see why the monk would chase me, but he did. I don't understand. For God's sake, he was a monk. Why would he be interested in a group of people who have been dead for ages?"

"Did he say anything to you?"

"Not really – wait. Aren't you supposed to be writing up a report about my home being broken into?"

"Yes. I'm trying to get both done. He had spoken to Gaetos about Luci and wasn't too sure about her innocent act. Gaetos had told him she thought Luci and the monk were friends. A little too convenient with the panic attack and being rushed away from the scene of the crime by ambulance so she couldn't be immediately interviewed. She would have time to get her thoughts and story straight, he thought.

She gasped. "Oh, I almost forgot. He said he wanted the diary that the boy had given me from my Uncle Nick. The monk said it belonged to the church."

"Well, does it?"

"No. It's a family heirloom. I recognized the cover. I was told by my grandfather that on my thirtieth birthday the book would be delivered to me."

"When the monk grabbed your arm, why didn't you just give it to him?" he asked as he pulled out photos from the crime scene and laid them before her."

"Why are you showing me these pictures? I saw what happened."

"Maybe you can remember something from the photos that you may have forgotten."

Luci looked closely and spotted where the monk had been impaled on the spikes. She counted and found there were ten. Ten meant something in the tarot cards, treason by a friend or family member, she remembered.

Max watched her. "Do you see anything?"

"No. Can you please take them away now?"

"Let me repeat, why didn't you just give the monk the diary?"

"It's mine. I'm not giving up something that my grandparents gave to me. I have very little left of my family. I wasn't about to let go of something that meant a lot for my grandfather to keep safe for me all these years."

"Some of the students said they thought he meant to hurt you. Did he?"

"When he grabbed me, I felt threatened, but the police arrived."

"Can you give me any idea why the monk would have wanted to take that book away from you?"

"As I stated, I have no clue. The person who wrote the diary wasn't Catholic, like the monk. She was a Cathar, a distant relative of mine who my grandfather wanted me to know about. It was her diary."

Luci felt a little uncomfortable talking to this police officer. He seemed to want to know too much about the book and not about someone in her home.

After what happened today, she couldn't be sure he wasn't after the diary. "The Cathars believed that the world was split along lines of matter and spirit, good and evil. They believed in purifying themselves, clean living, chastity, poverty, and equality of the sexes.

"The Cathars felt that everything materialistic was evil, and they considered all the trapping and rituals of the papacy evil. Their opposition to possessions endeared them to the poor and to the nobility in Languedoc, who had grown tired of the taxation by the church."

"I heard there were stories that the Knights Templar preserved some of the Cathar secrets and possibly some sacred artifact, like the Holy Grail or Solomon's treasure. Do you think he thought the book would give him a map to find the treasure?" he asked.

"Anyone who has studied the Inquisitions would think that."

"I just want to cover every angle. Dr Gaetos mentioned you still have the diary. Is it here?"

"No. I took it to the bank and left it in my safety deposit box. Why?"

"No reason. Gaetos thought the monk was after that diary."

Walking over to her backpack, which was on the kitchen table, she covered up the diary with a kitchen towel. She came back to the officer and handed him a book by Bishop Folques that she had been reading earlier. She wasn't sure why; maybe just a gut feeling, but she wasn't sure if she trusted him.

"Here. Maybe you can learn something about the Cathars from this book if you're interested."

Max held out his hand and, for just a moment, they touched again. Luci felt the warmth that he emanated. And, for a second time in less than a half hour, she sensed the heat rising to her face.

"I received the diary from a young man who found me in the library at the college. The monk knifed him, I believe. He was bleeding when I last saw him. I reported it to the campus police. Do you know if they found him? Is he okay?"

"I'm sorry. He was dead on the campus grounds when the police found him. Did you know him?"

"No. How sad. He was so young. I have no idea who he was," Luci said.

Max handed the Folques book back to Luci. "I don't think I'll need this, but thanks. Is there anything else you can think of that's related to the book the priest may have thought you had?"

"I can't think of anything in particular," she said, not telling him about the tarot cards."

"Dr Gaetos also said you would be leaving the country. Please give me your forwarding address. I don't know what this is all about, or why you're involved, but a murder has taken place, and I need to find out why." Max turned to leave and looked frustrated at her lack of cooperation.

"I haven't decided about leaving, but if I do, I'll fax my itinerary to you," she said, closing the door.

Max's phone rang as he stepped outside of Luci's home. "Max, I see you made a visit to our Luci. Keep away from her. There's a lot at stake and we will not hesitate to kill you or her."

The line went dead. Max got in his car and drove away.

A patrol car pulled up into the condominium complex and the officer in uniform walked up the driveway. He entered through the front gate into her garden and knocked on the front door.

Thinking it was Officer Dantie, Luci walked back and opened the door.

"Good evening, Ma'am. I'm here to take a report on a robbery."

Stunned, Luci told the officer what she had told the man she'd *thought* was a police officer. This officer called for an APB on the black SUV that Max had parked in her driveway.

"I'll be back to check on you, and there will be an officer policing the area in case he comes back."

"He wasn't a cop after all? What the hell is going on?" she asked herself after the officer left.

Walking back into her kitchen, she pulled a pair of gloves from a cabinet drawer and put them on before she picked up Esclarmonde's Diary. She wanted to protect the aging book.

According to the diary, the last Prefect of the Cathars was Corba de Foix, the sister of the nobleman, Raimond Roger, warlord of the Ariege. She was a strong woman and opposed the Roman Church and the French kings who coveted Occitan.

Having attended Yale, Luci knew that the Beinecke Rare Book and Manuscript Library at Yale University held many original manuscripts. She also knew that it held a copy of some of the original tarot cards. Somehow, she would have to get on an airplane and look at the original documents, and maybe even take Janet up on traveling to France.

The next day, driving out to the stables to see her horse, Zane, before driving to San Jose to fly to her old alma mater, Luci made a copy of Esclarmonde's entire diary at an office store, then put the original in a safe deposit bank at the Educational Employees' Bank. She would mail individual sections of the diary to herself at Yale University, and to other places where the diary might lead her. By sending individual chapters, if someone were trying to get the diary away from her, she wouldn't have the complete book on her.

She then went to the bank to her safe deposit box but before leaving, she went to a teller and withdrew some cash. Arriving home, she sat down at her computer and looked up the Magician tarot card, and found that it meant "to conquer nature."

Before going to bed, she poured herself a glass of wine and thought of all the strange coincidences that were piling up. It had something to do with Esclarmonde's diary and involved whoever was leaving tarot cards for her. Were they messages of some kind, directing her somewhere? The only way she would ever know about her family and possibly the sacred artefact was to get on that plane tomorrow.

"I think I'll call in my prescription to the drug store. I'm going to need some Clonazepam to get me through all of this."

Esclarmonde's Diary

June, 1209

Aunt Corba had become a Prefect of the Cathars and I had taken her place as High Priestess. Aunt Corba sent me to meet with the Knight Templar who was to protect her.

I left to meet up with the knight to test his skills. He is to guard my aunt and yet I feel that I am the better protector.

I set out on my white steed wearing the pax tablet, engraved on one side with two robed figures in an embrace, accompanied by a marking of an esoteric alphabet. The other side holds a triple cross, the sign of the Cathars. He will know me by this identification.

Two leagues after I left Montsegur, I saw wisps of dust that impeded my view in the daylight. It was from a traveler on horseback heading my way on an Arabian horse. The knight identified himself as a Templar by brandishing his shield with the white cross heraldry.

I did not waiver and continued heading straight for him. I was anxious to see him. He lifted his shield a second time for good measure. I spurred my horse forward, rising and sinking across the valley floor.

The knight nodded and when I approached, I jumped off my horse and ran straight for him. The knight swung his leg over his horse and readied for the attack he thought was coming. A few paces from collision, I threw off my helmet. Guilhelm had not recognized me but when he did, we fell into each other's arms. Delighted, I laughed at his surprise and we fell to the ground in laughter.

"I had hoped you were the one being sent to see me at Montsegur," I said. "It has been a long time, Guilhelm."

Long ago, Guilhelm had turned his feelings away from me because of his calling and because knights were married to their cause, not to women. I knew he loved me as I loved him. But it was not to be in this lifetime. He looked at me with desire as he helped me back onto my horse without a word. We rode side-by-side, on to Montsegur.

Guilhelm told me that not even the description of the holy places in the Bible could have prepared him for the incredible view that Montsegur offered. Riding together toward the towering mount of Montsegur was like watching an eruption of a volcano among fields of sheep and oak groves. The mount looked like the head of a god who had long ago fallen from the sky to land on the earth. The summit was sharp like the surrounding Pyrenean caps, but rounded like a ball, and the pitch on all three sides was so severe no vegetation could grow. I was happy to share this with him.

I let him know we would have to travel by foot to get through the upcoming pass. As we walked, leaves and old twigs crackled underfoot.

Guilhelm followed me up the switchback and I wondered anew why he was coming with me when he was born a Roman and I, a Cathar. When the side of the mountain became steeper, I extended my hand for assistance. He hesitated and cast his eyes down. I noticed he recognized the pax necklace around my neck.

His fingers trembled slightly as he pulled me up the precipice.

He was becoming quite uncomfortable. I could see we would never be alone together after this meeting.

It was a time of insanity. All Cathars were in danger. Guilhelm was sent to Montsegur to defend the Prefect and the High Priestess with his life.

"I will protect the secret of the tarot on this pax tablet," I said.

While there was still sunlight, Guilhelm and I made up an alphabet known only to one another. We pledged to protect the secret hideaway of the treasure.

After completing the task, I slowly took off my brother's armor. Underneath, I was wearing a simple shirt and leggings. I noticed that Guilhelm glanced at my breasts pushing against the damp fabric of my shirt. He became aroused and I could see in his eyes that he wanted to touch me. I wanted him and moved closer to his outstretched hands, just this one time for we might never be together again. He removed my clothing, and cradled me as we lay on the ground. He pushed into me, slowly at first, feeling his way for I was his first woman. I wanted this moment to last forever.

He took my hand in his, and, together we watched the sun crest over the mountain and breathed in the rich, earthly smell of leaf and moss.

The Star

Think of yourself as an incandescent power, illuminated perhaps,
forever talked to by God and his messengers.
~ Brenda Ueland

Luci aged 30
San Jose International Airport was a city-owned, public-use airport serving the county of Santa Clara, not far from Monterey, California.

Luci had prepared herself for her journey, one Clonazepam, and her daily dose of Wellbutrin. Check-in was quick and efficient, but when it came time to scan her bags, she encountered a problem. The TSA agent stopped her to go through her purse. He was having a problem with her small pink container in one of the side pockets of her purse and wanted to send it back through security. After sending it back through the second time, he still felt it was suspicious.

Motioning toward the pocket, the TSA agent told Luci, "I need you to take the container out of your purse and put it on the counter."

Luci complied, removing the pink plastic container.

By then, all personnel and passengers were watching with concern. Luci would have been nervous if it hadn't been so funny.

She watched the TSA agent as he opened up the container and pulled out the contents of the pink container to reveal a Tampax.

"Does this look like it's going to be a problem or would you like to check it out for yourself?"

Embarrassed, he turned a bright red. "Thank you, you can go."

Luci smiled politely, grabbed her purse, put her shoes on, and headed for the flight that would take her to New Haven, Connecticut.

After a glass of wine before boarding, she slept until the hostess announced their arrival in Philadelphia. Once they landed, she would have to race to the US Air terminal to catch her flight to Tweed Airport in New Haven. She boarded the flight moments before they shut the door. Sitting down, she asked the airline hostess for a sewing kit. She had brought her teddy bear for security and she needed to sew it together.

Luci took her bear out of her purse. It seemed silly to bring the bear, but this was what her mom had given her just before her death. Fingering the hole, she felt something hard inside, and became curious. She couldn't believe it. Her bear had held something from her mom for all these years. She reached deep inside the bear's stomach and pulled out a tiny note with a key. It was difficult to read as tears were streaming down her face.

My darling Luci, if you are reading this then your dad and I are gone. Your grandparents will come and care for you and they will leave you with a very important diary written by a Cathar. Follow the diary and tarot cards. They will lead you to the truth. Be careful, my darling daughter; others will be searching for this treasure. I leave you with the lullaby that I sang to you as a child and played for you on the musical box your grandparents had sent you.

Through her tears, she sewed the note and the key back inside the bear, remembering long ago when she'd seen her mom place the key there and the Occitan lullaby, "Som Som" that her mother had sung to her. She hummed the lullaby softly, remembering her mother.

Sleep, Sleep
Sleep, sleep, come, come, come,
Sleep, sleep, come from somewhere.
Sleep, sleep, come, come, come,
Sleep, Sleep, come from somewhere.
The sleep doesn't want to come,
The little child doesn't want to sleep.

The sleep went away,
Riding a goat,
I'll be back tomorrow,
Riding a foal.

Come from the vineyards,

To lull the girls to sleep.
Come from the firesides,
To lull the little boys to sleep.

Mummy is by the fire,
She's baking a cake.
Daddy is bringing a bird,
In the hollow of his hat.

After reading her mom's note, Luci felt more resolved than ever to retrieve the Cathar codex that Esclarmonde and Loup had left for her family.

Leaving the terminal after arrival, she hopped on a bus for the rental car booth where she had pre-paid for a car. On the display monitor, she saw her name and rolled her luggage down the lanes of cars looking for aisle A6. After inspecting the car for dings and finding none, she climbed into a blue SUV.

Stopping at the booth to exit the airport, she handed her ticket and packet to a man who raised the bar so she could drive out. Leaving the airport, Luci drove down Burr Street onto 337th, past East Shore Park, and jumped onto I-95, the Connecticut Turnpike to Yale. She reached the center of Yale Universities in Hewitt Quadrangle, more commonly referred to as Beinecke Plaza. The building, designed by architect Gordon Bunshaft, was the largest building in the world reserved exclusively for the preservation of rare books and manuscripts.

† † †

Luci was amazed at how nostalgic she felt seeing her old alma mater. It reminded her of the last day she'd seen her grandparents and what they had wished for her. After parking her car, she reached into the back seat, swung her oversized purse out, and almost knocked over a man taking a picture on the sidewalk. She looked up and realized he was trying to take a shot of the translucent Danby marble. It was transferring subdued light against the evening sky. The way it lit up the sky, it looked like a beacon, beckoning her to this very place and time. She could understand why he was taking this shot.

"Shit, oh excuse me, I didn't see you," she said, reaching out to steady him.

"No, I'm sorry. I wasn't paying any attention. Look. *Amazing, isn't it?*"

Peering into the camera lens, she answered, "Yes, it's amazing. You have captured the essence of the stars transmitting light on the marble quite incredibly. Thank you for allowing me to see such a beautiful sight. I wish I could stay longer to observe your work. Please excuse me," Luci said, rushing away.

It was nearly five p.m. when she hurried down one of the two floors that extended under Hewitt Quadrangle. The first level was centered around a sunken courtyard featuring sculptures by Isamu Noguchi that were said to represent time – the pyramid, sun – the circle, and change – the cube. After walking down the stairs, she headed for the first unoccupied table, placed her backpack and writing tablet down, then made her way to the information dcsk.

A man slid out of his chair and collided with Luci as she was approaching the counter.

† † †

"Oh, excuse me," Father Del Pierro said, frowning down at her.

He had hoped to keep his distance from Luci, even though he doubted she'd recognize him after all these years.

"No problem," she said.

Wow, that is a handsome man. Where has he been my whole life?

† † †

Del Pierro left quickly out the front door in search of Luci's blue SUV. He popped the lock discreetly and placed a tracking device in the pocket lining of her luggage.

By the time Luci got to the information counter, it was getting late. Half the lights were out and only one librarian remained. A slightly plump, ginger-haired young woman was standing behind the desk. She was reading a book on economics. Luci's footsteps made her look up.

"Can I help you?" she asked.

"Haley," Luci addressed her, looking at her name tag. "I need to look at the original tarot cards written by the Cathars. I believe they were written on lambskin."

Clearly bored, Haley crossed the room to a wall of file cabinets. Out came a two-inch thick print-out which she set on her pristine desktop and flipped through.

According to Haley, Luci needed to walk over to the Old Library – now Dwight Hall – where she could find what she was looking for.

"What time does it close?" Luci asked

"Ahh, now," she said with sarcasm.

Damn, Luci thought. She would have to wait until eight tomorrow morning before she could see the tarot sheets. Disappointed, she left.

† † †

Hayley turned off the computer and went to the employee's lounge where she had left her sweater and purse in a locked cabinet. She felt very guilty about leading the Californian on a wild goose chase. She'd seemed like a decent person.

The man who had come earlier had said she was a colleague he was competing with on a research paper. He wanted to play a practical joke on her. Well, Haley thought, people have their different senses of humor. All she knew was that he had asked her out and let her choose the most expensive restaurant to have dinner together. Leaving the doorway, she rounded the corner and spotted her date for the evening at the rare books section. He must be returning the tarot cards that the Californian had requested. Haley didn't know much about him, except that he was tall, gorgeous, and had incredibly dark black eyes.

"Hey, beautiful," he said, smiling.

As he came closer, Del Pierro moved to put his arm around her. They left the library together toward her car.

Hayley was very excited. She would show Charlotte, the host at the restaurant, that she wasn't a bore. An intelligent, good-looking man was taking her out to dinner. Would Charlotte be jealous or what?

It was getting late and they would have to hurry to get to the restaurant in time. In the parking lot, Hayley gestured toward the red Kia and turned toward her vehicle to unlock the door. Turning swiftly back to him, she asked, "Does the Four Seasons work for you?"

†††

That's all the time she had to say anything. From his waistband, he slipped out his gun with an attached silencer and double-tapped her in the middle of her forehead. Haley slumped to the ground, with little red clots weeping blood down her face.

Stepping over her body, he leaned in close and said, "Not tonight, honey. You're really not my type anyway. I have another young woman who I've wanted to have for a very long time."

He didn't need a witness tracing the tarot cards he'd stolen from the library. Maybe the police would think a gang member had shot her as part of an initiation.

The Popess

Jesus composed a more spiritual gospel for the use of those who were being perfected ... to be read by those who were being guided toward the path of the Angels.
~ Cathars

Hungry and disappointed, Luci walked back to her rental car and found a hotel called the Premiere Hotel and Suites that was within her budget. Lifting her bag out of the car, she felt someone watching her from the parking lot. She was becoming more paranoid, if that was possible.

It was getting dark, and the street light cast a shadow across a man's face in the parking lot of the hotel. Luci found herself staring at him. He wore a Red Sox baseball hat and waved at her, relieving her anxiety. Locking the car door, she rolled her luggage to the entrance of the hotel. The lovely gatehouse opened up to the hub of the hotel. From where she was standing, she could smell the food as she entered the main lobby and her stomach responded accordingly, much to her embarrassment.

Luci handed her ID over to the desk clerk and he had the key and room ready for her in minutes.

Luci picked up her bags and, with key in hand, left the front counter toward the restaurant, she was starving. Sipping a glass of white wine, she sat back and ordered a Caesar salad and a medium rare steak with loads of onions. She was entranced by the smell and taste of her food and noticed a middle-aged gentleman with perfectly creased trousers coming toward her. He was the guy who had been taking pictures at Yale library.

"Hello," he said with an engaging smile, reaching over to shake her hand. "We seem to keep bumping into one another."

Surprised, Luci looked up from her food and grinned. "Sorry. I didn't notice you standing there. I do, however, remember nearly knocking you over in front of the library."

"Yes, you were pretty engrossed," he said. "Can I sit with you? I hate eating alone. By the way, my name is Nick. Are you from California? From your apparel it seems so. Well, so am I. I just arrived at Yale to do research at the library when I first saw you."

"Oh," she said. "My name is Luci. Please, sit with me," she said with just a little trepidation. "What are you doing your research on, Nick?"

Before he answered, he asked a waiter to bring a bottle of Cru wine from the San Joaquin Valley in California.

"Okay, where exactly are you from?" Luci asked. "Because I don't know too many people on this side of the United States who know about Cru wine."

"I was born in France. My family traveled extensively. When I was very young, I moved to Fresno, California, about thirty minutes from the Cru Winery. Where are you from?" he asked.

"This really is a small world. I live in Pacific Grove and work at the college about three hours from you, but I guess you're familiar with Monterey." *How incredible*, Luci thought. She felt very comfortable with Nick and was glad to have some company while eating dinner.

"I go there every chance I can," he said with a grin. "I really like the atmosphere. I also work at a university, but in Fresno. I have been there since the program began in 1956, when it was under the Enology, Food Science, and Nutrition Department. We grew into a one-of-a-kind program that became recognized throughout the world."

"I've heard of it. Your school has won some awards and created a wine for the Poet Laureate, Peter Levine, hasn't it?"

They began discussing the research they were doing in their fields of expertise. It was getting late and Luci, worn out from the last few days and all the wine she had been consuming, stifled a yawn. "Sorry, it's not the company. I'm just tired. I need to get to my room. I have an early morning." After paying for her dinner, she got up from her chair and excused herself from the table. "It has certainly been an enjoyable evening, and if you ever get to Monterey, give me a call," she said, handing him her business card.

"Thank you, Luci." Nick smiled. He got up, reached over the table to shake her hand, and took the card. "Until we meet again."

† † †

Nick, unbeknownst to Luci, had kept watch over her ever since his sister, Luci's mother, had been killed in the car crash. Few people knew of him or were aware that he had kept Esclarmonde's diary safe until Luci reached her thirtieth birthday. He was part of the Cathar faith and the members were confident that Luci would be able to find the lost treasure. They thought she could restore the artefact taken from them so long ago. They also believed she was the High Priestess of the Cathars, foretold in the tarot cards because she was the direct descendant of Esclarmonde.

Nick had sent the diary to Luci through a fellow Cathar many years after his parents' death in the fire. He felt confident that no one knew about him and too many years had passed for anyone to remember Luci as an adult from *The Order*. He had always stayed a safe distance away from her. Now, his friend whom he sent to the library to give the diary to Luci was dead. Nick felt responsible. His niece was not safe, and neither was he.

Nick had been fooling himself thinking no one would be looking for the artefact after all these years. That it was a myth. But things had taken a turn for the worse. He had begun to watch Janet Gaetos from afar and had hacked into her computer.' Nick found some puzzling coincidences about Luci's boss and they worried him. He'd decided to contact Luci and protect her.

Letting go of his hand, Luci looked up at Nick and smiled. She left the restaurant and went up the escalator to her room. Putting the plastic card through the door lock wasn't easy. She never knew what end you had to put in first, and she was always carrying a purse, her laptop, and her suitcases which made it impossible to open the damn door. After several failed attempts, Luci entered her room and noticed an envelope resting on the nightstand next to the television set that had her name on it.

Opening it, she pulled out the Popess, another tarot card. Luci's hands began to shake. Nervously, she looked around to see if there was anyone else in the room. She didn't have Louie or a baseball bat this time.

Luci called down to the front desk and asked if someone had sent a note to her room.

"Yes," the hotel operator said. "A letter was given to the front desk to be delivered to your room."

"Thank you," Luci said, hanging up the phone. She just couldn't seem to shake these cards and whoever was sending them to her.

Luci grew up thinking the tarot cards were on the same level as witchcraft, the Ouija board, and astrology. All she could think of was that something was very wrong, and someone was sending her a message via tarot cards. Grabbing her iPhone, she dialed Sarah. She had to let her know the latest information.

"Good morning, Sarah. Sorry to wake you. How's Louie doing?"

"Misses you. Hey, what time is it?" she asked. "Shit, Luci couldn't you have waited two more hours to call me? I'm really beginning to hate you."

"Really didn't think about it. Thought you might be interested to know that I received another card. This time, it's the Popess."

"So what?"

"Well, according to Wikipedia, there was a popess named Joan. This is probably when the Italian pope fled Rome to France for safety."

"So this Joan becomes the popess of Rome, really?"

"Yep, historically there is no evidence of there ever being a popess, but there is a legend of a female pope who became popular in 1099, during a time when there were several anti-popes who challenged the authority of Rome. Legend has it that Pope Joan became pregnant and delivered a child during a procession through the city, revealing her identity as a woman. She was publicly stoned to death. Although the legend might not be supported by fact, it did have a significant cultural impact. In 1601, Pope Clement VIII may have inadvertently given the story a degree of credibility by officially declaring it to be untrue. To the mass of believers, the legend of Pope Joan became an anti-papal satire and survived as a political slur against the official pope. The church seemed to grow and prosper under her reign. The Popess indicates a heretical theme and implies a direct challenge to the pope's authority. It was very curious that this card was included in the tarot and left in an envelope for me."

"What does it say?"

"It's more what it shows. The woman in the card is wearing a brown robe and a three-tiered tiara, just like the pope."

"Was she on the same level as the pope?"

"Let me find out." Picking up her laptop, Luci looked up the definition of the Popess card. "It says here that the card represents the dualistic nature of man and woman. On her lap, the Popess holds an open book, which seems to challenge the church's explanation of God's secret plan, which is revealed only at the final judgment. Here, with the Popess holding the book, it seems to tell us that the information in the book is available to all, not just a select few in the hierarchy of the church."

Luci held the card between her fingers, spinning it around, searching her memory. The Empress was supposed to represent the female matriarch of France, but maybe it represented someone else in history.

"Luci, are you still there?"

"Yeah, sorry, got caught up in all of this. Wait, I have to go," she said excitedly. "Someone is turning the knob on my hotel door. I'm calling the front desk."

"Maybe it's just the maid bringing chocolate."

"No, they would knock first and there was no one knocking."

Luci slammed down the phone and watched as the doorknob turned again. She wasn't taking any chances. Quietly walking over to the door, she looked out the spyglass. She didn't recognize the man. He was wearing a Red Sox baseball cap. She ran back to the phone and called the front desk. "Someone is trying to break into my room. Please send Security, hurry!"

"What?" the kid said. "Are you sure?"

"Of course, I'm sure. I can see him from the peephole. Isn't that why the hotel puts them in?" The kid was not taking her seriously, so Luci screamed, "Get someone up here before something happens to me!"

"Okay, Dr de Foix, I'll send our guard up. But you really don't need to worry. It's probably someone lost, drunk, or just got the wrong room."

"Look, you little prick, get someone up to my room right now, or I'll have your balls in a vice as soon as I get out of here." She packed up her bags and sat, watching the door, waiting, hopefully, for the guard.

Luci heard someone running down the hall. Looking through the spyglass, she saw the hotel Security approaching.

"We have another room on a secure floor for you, Dr de Foix. Please pack up your belongings and come with us," he said.

She picked up her things and left the room with the two burly men. Looking around, she didn't see anyone in the hallway, but noticed the stairwell door was slightly ajar. The men quietly took her to a penthouse suite with a key that was used for access to the penthouse level. Surveying the room, she felt a little safer than she had in her other room. Luci kept her bags packed, took a shower, and went to bed in her clothes, just in case the prowler came looking for her.

† † †

He saw Luci leaving her room with Security and go to the penthouse. He couldn't possibly get up to the top floor at that short notice. *No accidental fall from the balcony here.* Unfortunately, his business with Dr de Foix would have to wait. He could be patient.

He walked outside the hotel entrance and lit a cigarette. He hated the new filtered ones. Give him an old-fashioned Camel and he was satisfied. He sat in his car, smoking, and waiting for the lovely Luci.

† † †

Luci tossed and turned in her sleep. She got up and retrieved the copied version of Esclarmonde's diary. At five a.m., she left the hotel with her bags, and drove to a twenty-four-hour diner to wait for the Yale library to open. She was right about Esclarmonde's book. It didn't hold all the clues that she was looking for. She needed to see the original copies of the tarot.

Death

*Reflect upon your present blessings of which every man has plenty,
not on your past misfortunes of which all men have some.*
~ Charles Dickens

Entering the Yale campus, Luci saw police cars surrounding the library. She parked toward a marque. She had been correct and the tarot cards were, indeed, in the Beinecke Library.

Luci went to the front desk and asked if there were any copies of the tarot cards. The elderly librarian directed her to the bottom floor of the library where Lucy began her research into the Cathars' use of the tarot. According to the text on tarot cards, no one knew the exact date when the first tarot originated. Luci found a copy of one of the earliest forms of tarot card, similar to the Marseilles style, in what was called the Cary Yale sheet – an uncut sheet of images housed in the Beinecke Rare Book Manuscript Library. According to Thylbus, a scholar on tarot, Cathars and gypsies passed on secrets and knowledge that had been suppressed by the Catholic Church. Hence, the reason why the church condemned the tarot cards and considered them evil to this day. In the centuries that followed, the tarot was circulated by travelling entertainers and gypsies.

Gypsies roamed from France to the Middle East. They knew exactly what the cards were. They had heard about the codex given to Mary Magdalene by Jesus and knew the cards held the secrets of the Sacred Book of the Angels where the fifth anti-Christ is revealed. The gypsies were able to continue spreading the true word of Jesus without the Roman Church becoming suspicious. People from around the countryside would come to the gypsies' campsite to be entertained and have their fortunes told. The remaining families of the Cathars went to find out what had happened to their kin and to keep in touch with their religion.

The tarot consisted of the Minor Arcana, four suits called swords, cups, pentacles, and scepters, and the Major Arcana or Great Secrets, known as trumps. Among the trumps was the Joker, which had survived in modern playing cards. The joker, or the "fool," was the one who used humor and clowning around to pass on the message of Christ. Were the gypsies the fools in the deck, she wondered, and if so, what message have they been passing, knowingly or unknowingly throughout the ages?

Peering closely at the Cary-Yale sheet, she saw that the Joker was the last card of the tarot, numbered zero. *Did people consider the gypsies the wandering preachers, practising poverty? Are these the people whom the Apostle Paul referred to as fools for Christ?*

The French word "le Mat" could mean checkmate, beaten, or vanquished. This could be said of the gypsies. But it could also refer to the remaining Cathars after their defeat at the hands of the Roman Church and then another devil.

Luci walked back up the flight of stairs of the Beinecke Library. It was very quiet as she ascended, and thought the students would be arriving. She tried to organize her thoughts and wondered about the dead monk and his connection to all that had happened. She knew she needed to call Janet to let her know she was going to France for her and the benefactor who had given the college the grant. She could research the symbols on the Major Arcana in France to see where they led and to work on the five-million dollar project.

As Luci headed out the front door of the Beinecke Library, something burst from one of the top-floor windows of the library. She stared up as a body was ejected headfirst, flipped in midair, and then slammed down on top of a black sedan.

She raced toward the vehicle and recognized the man. Nick, the man she had dinner with last night. Screaming for help, she saw people dialing their phones. She picked up Nick's wrist. There was a pulse, very faint, but he was still alive. Amazingly, Nick opened his eyes.

"Can you hear me?" she asked him.

Faintly, he beckoned her to come closer.

Luci moved closer to hear what he could tell her.

"I'm sorry, Luci. I was supposed to protect you. Keep your teddy bear close. He holds the key and trust no one. I'm your uncle, Nick," he whispered. "Follow the diary and the tarot. It will lead you to the Cathar codex and your destiny."

Something whizzed past Luci's head and slammed into the windshield on her left side. Warm blood spattered her clothing from the shards of glass hitting her and Nick. Luci noticed a shadow in the mirror of the left side window. A man with a gun stood there. Luci couldn't see him clearly, but he was wearing a baseball cap, the same one the man had worn who'd tried to enter her hotel room last night.

She froze, looking back down at Nick. She saw his chest rise and fall, then someone touched her shoulder. She hadn't realized she was screaming. When she looked up, she saw Max Dantie. She couldn't believe her eyes.

He leaned over. "Calm down, Luci," he whispered. "The church knows you're after the secret of the Cathars, and it must be vital to them. I know you're headed for France. You need to get out of here as quickly as you can and head for the airport. Take British Air to Charles de Gaulle Airport. There is a flight leaving tonight. I'll join you as quickly as I can. Don't call anyone. Do you understand me?"

Through her tears, she saw that Dantie was serious about her leaving. But she was a witness. "Won't the police want to speak to me?"

"No cops."

Max's reaction might not have been what she'd been hoping for, but it wasn't a surprise. Luci wasn't quite sure how to proceed anyway. She had never been in this kind of situation before.

"Don't you think there've been enough dead bodies? Get out of here or you won't be able to get to France. You'll be dead. I'll cover everything here."

She knew she needed to get out of there. Luci stumbled because her legs felt rubbery, as if they belonged to someone else. He grabbed hold of her and kept her steady. Looking up at him, she saw the beginnings of a smile touch his mouth, while a decided twinkle brightened his eyes. Max was helping her to relax and get away, but all she could see were his eyes. They were the deep blue color of the ocean. She realized it was the first time she'd actually looked at them in enough light to notice. She had thought they were plain blue before. He reminded her of a boy she'd fought in a Kung Fu match long ago.

But that was impossible. Wasn't it?

"Now go, Luci, as quickly as you can without garnering any more attention. People are looking at him, not at you."

Slowly, Luci walked behind a blue convertible then just sat behind the vehicle, shaking. She needed to calm down. She couldn't have a panic attack now; she had to get her pills in her suitcase. She raced back to the parking lot and jumped into her SUV. On the passenger seat was the Death card. She nervously picked it up, threw it into her purse, then began driving slowly so as not to arouse any suspicion. She saw police and an ambulance as their sirens screamed past her to take Nick to the hospital.

Luci drove her SUV to the home of her old college professor to retrieve a copy of the diary from him then began to snake her way behind cars down Edgewood Avenue away from Nick. She was now involved in murder if he died, but she prayed Nick survived.

Twenty yards away, she glanced back and saw Dantie talking to a police officer and pointing in her direction. Confused, she stood up and ran, turning the corner at York Street, using the college buildings as a shield against anyone who chose to pursue her. Blood pumped throughout her body, her head hurt, but she wanted to live. And getting away from the baseball-hat man and Dantie was something she had to do. And he seemed to know her every move. She didn't know who to trust anymore.

She thought about calling Sarah to ask her for help, but remembered Nick's warning, maybe they were able to track her whereabouts. She rounded another building, dropped down a stairwell, and knelt to gulp some air into her lungs. Sirens were racing down the street toward her. She dug into her purse, pulled out a scarf, tied it around her hair, then turned her reversible jacket inside out to hide Nicholas's blood. Climbing back up the stairs, she headed for the train station in a cab. She wanted to take the British Air jet to Charles de Gaulle. Dantie would not have seen her watching as he pointed the police in her direction.

In the cab, she took out her purse and swallowed a Clonazepam, and stole another look at the Death card. There was a crescent moon behind the skeleton, turned 180 degrees, and it implied evil. Who was the evil person in her life?

"Is Dantie or Gaetos after me? The Red Sox man – what part does he play in all of this besides trying to murder me?" she wondered aloud.

"What?" the cab driver said.

"Nothing, just changed my mind about something." After hitting New York, she decided, she'd take Air France to Scotland. That was where the Rosslyn Chapel was and where many of the Knights Templar were murdered.

The Magician in the tarot deck was the first card, the starting point in a journey. Her journey. Whatever treasure was out there, she was going to get it.

Earlier, at a Fed Ex she had retrieved another of the copies of Esclarmonde's diary she had made and sent to her old college instructor. Now it was time to go to the post office and mail the copy to Scotland.

The Knave

Blessed is he who stands at the beginning.
That one will know the end ...
~ The Gospel of Thomas

Luci boarded Air France without any more mishaps and didn't notice anyone following her when she arrived in Scotland. Hailing a taxi, she made her way to Rosslyn Chapel. She was amazed at the beautiful, ornate fifteenth-century medieval chapel near Edinburgh.

She walked up the stairs of the cathedral and entered through the front door. She noticed they had guided tours and walked over to where a young man who looked like a college student was giving them. He had a cute Scottish brogue, which made the excursion even more interesting.

† † †

Father Del Pierro was never far from Luci, having placed the tracking device in her suitcase when she had arrived at the Premiere Hotel. After all these years, things were all beginning to come together. Earlier, he had hacked into her computer and, before long, he would have the codex and the treasure. All he had to do was get rid of the competition and wait for his opportunity, he thought, placing his favorite baseball team cap in his coat pocket. Janet had not gotten to Luci yet. He didn't know what her game was, but he'd be damned if he'd let her get in his way. The next time they met, she would get more than powder burns.

† † †

"Over here, Ms de Foix," the tour guide said. "Rosslyn Chapel's proper name is the Collegiate Chapel of St Mathew and it was founded on a hill above Rosslyn Glen as a Catholic collegiate church in the mid-thirteenth century. It is renowned for its famous stone carvings, some of the finest in Europe, and many of which relate to the symbolism of the Old Testament, Freemasonry, and the biblical Apocrypha."

"Was this chapel built by the Knights Templar?"

"We know that the chapel was founded by Sir William St Clair or Sinclair, first Earl of Caithness of the Sinclair family – a noble family, descended in part from Norman knights from the commune of Saint-Clair-Sur-Epte in northern France. He used the designs the medieval architects made available to him, but the original plans for Rosslyn have never been found or recorded, so it is open to speculation whether or not the chapel was intended to be built in its current design. Many speculate that he was a Knight Templar. Back then, one did not freely admit to being one. Rosslyn Chapel is only part of what it was originally intended to be. Many believe it was supposed to be a larger cruciform in shape. It was never completed. Only the choir was constructed, with the retro-chapel, otherwise called the Lady Chapel, which was built on the much earlier crypt. That was believed to be an earlier castle. The building has a tower, not unlike the Chartres Cathedral in France. Though incomplete, it took forty years to build and has the largest number of Green Man carvings of any medieval chapel in Europe."

"I've never heard of a lady chapel."

"Mary Magdalene was basically forced out of Jerusalem by Peter, many suspect, and was sent, rudderless, in a boat to France. Most churches are named after Mary or Mary of Magdalene in France. She's believed to be originally from Nigeria. That's why she's called the Black Madonna. Now let me tell you about the pillars," said the guide. "They are supposed to represent the pillars of Boza and Jachin. They stood at the inner porchway of Solomon's Temple in Jerusalem. This chapel is a reproduction of that temple. According to historical documents, some of the Knights Templar who escaped France joined other orders. Many scholars are studying the carvings in this chapel to see if the Knights Templar not only helped to build it, but also hid, with the help of Sir William St Clair, the knights' treasure that came from Solomon's Temple."

Luci walked over to a dusty wall that was engraved with a saying. "*Non nobis Domine, non nobis, sed nomini tuo da gloriam,*" she murmured.

"Over here, the three pillars at the east end of the chapel are named, from north to south, the Master Pillar, the Journeyman Pillar, and, most famously, the Apprentice Pillar."

"What is the meaning behind the names?" A young tourist asked.

"Well, the Apprentice Pillar got its name from a legend dating from the eighteenth century story, involving the master mason in charge of the stonework in the chapel and his young apprentice. According to legend, the master mason did not believe the apprentice could perform the complicated task of carving the column without seeing the original which formed the inspiration for the design. The master mason traveled to see the original himself in St Chartres. When he returned, he became enraged to find the apprentice had completed the column anyway. In a fit of rage, the mason took up his mallet and hit the apprentice on the head, killing him. The legend concludes that as punishment for his crime the master mason's face was carved into the opposite corner to forever gaze upon his apprentice's pillar."

"Serves him right. Now tell me about the Green Man carvings. What are they?" A young female tourist exclaimed.

"They are pagan figures. The vines that sprout from their mouths represent nature's growth, renewal, and fertility, illustrating the unity between humankind and nature."

"There seem to be quite a few of them. I guess they were a very fertile people," a pot-bellied American man joked.

Missing the joke, the guide added, "In Rosslyn, the Green Men are found in all areas of the chapel, with one example in the Lady Chapel, between the two middle altars of the east wall. In all, there are a hundred and ten carvings of Green Men."

"I heard that the Rosslyn Chapel is a repository for many artefacts, including the Lost Scrolls of the Temple, the Ark of the Covenant, the Holy Grail, and the true Stone of Destiny."

"Yes, we've all heard that, but if they are, we haven't found them. But I'll keep looking," he said, laughing. "Take a look over here at the musical boxes."

"What is the importance?" asked Luci.

"Among Rosslyn's many carvings are a sequence of two hundred and thirteen cubes – or boxes – protruding from the pillars and arches with a selection of patterns on them. It is still unknown whether these patterns have any meaning or are a cypher of some sort."

"My God, I wonder if it does have some meaning?" she said softly.

"What?"

"Oh, sorry, just mumbling to myself," Luci said.

Continuing his monologue, he waved his hand. "Now over here, this object is called a *pax tablet*. Most were tablets made of gold or bronze. This one was simple and was worn as some sort of ornament or decoration," he said, pointing to a glass enclosure.

"Is there any indication that would suggest that the Cathars came here?"

"The only written words in this chapel are 'Kings are strong, wine is stronger, women are stronger still – but, strongest of all, is Truth.' Women were very powerful in the Cathar religion and closely attached to the Knights Templar. Are you interested in the Cathars?"

"Yes, I have been doing research for a class I teach in California," she told him. "I'm also a relative of one of the women who was a High Priestess during the Albignesian War. There is a document that was given to the Cathars that spoke of the Knights Templar, gypsies, and St Chartres in France."

"I have seen St Chartres and there is a window called the Rose Window in the North Portal. I think you might want to look there for your research. It's where the Cathars' history is supposed to be. I think you might find clues to what you're looking for. Most of the history of St Chartres is lost and will take years or an order from the church."

"What's that?" questioned Luci.

"It's a special document to allow certain researchers to excavate in St Chartres. They have tried for years to dig down under the cathedral, but it hasn't happened yet. I wish you the best of luck, Luci."

Luci walked out of Rosslyn Chapel and decided that, somehow, she would have to get an even better look at the *pax tablet* and find out the meaning of the Latin words. It might have a clue.

She walked back to her hotel and got her laptop out of her travel bag. Later in the day, she looked up the words written on the dusty wall of the museum. "*Non nobis Domine, non nobis, sed nomini tuo da gloriam.*" She knew she had seen this before; they were in the diary. It meant *Not to us, o Lord, not to us, but to Thy name be Thy honor.*

That was the motto of the Knights Templar. Luci knew the Templars, and their secrets might still be there.

† † †

Just before the museum closed, Luci headed back toward Rosslyn Chapel. She was relieved to see that the person at the counter selling tickets was an elderly lady bundled up in a sweater because of the cold draft wafting through the museum. Luci bought a ticket from her.

"Would you like a guided tour?"

"Thank you, but no. I just want to wander around by myself, if that's okay with you."

"Of course it is. Just remember, we close at five o'clock, right on the dot."

"I promise I'll watch the time."

Luci immediately went past the Green Man figures to the glass enclosure. From her purse, she pulled out her phone and took several pictures of the peculiar writing. Stepping back, she bumped into something. Turning, she spotted the seal of the Knights Templar: two riders on a single horse.

Luci had a moment of inspiration and raced back to the musical boxes. She located the song her mother used to sing to her online and played the sound near the boxes. With the end of the last chord, a drawer opened up and another tarot card popped out – the Knave card, a message of love, confidence, and collaborator.

In the distance, she could hear the tour guide walking her way with a tourist group.

†††

Not far behind Luci, hidden behind a half wall, Del Pierro had been watching. He wondered what she was doing. It was time for him to call Cardinal Saachio. He enjoyed watching the sway of her hips. "Not long, Luci; it won't be long," he whispered.

Madman-Strangeness

This is the very perfection of man, to find out his own imperfections.
~ Saint Augustine

Cardinal Saachios' job as a diplomat was normally occupied by a career diplomat. He had no experience working in the church's diplomatic corps, which managed its international relations and was part of the *administratia.* Saachio selected Nathaniel Del Pierro and Fedrico Verase, his cousins from the streets of Calabria, to be his spies within the Vatican walls. Their families, unbeknownst to the church, were part of the 'Ndrangheta, onorata societa – honored society.

The 'Ndrangheta recruited members on the criterion of blood relationships, resulting in an extraordinary cohesion within the family clan. This presented major obstacles for the capture and conviction of these men.

There was money to be laundered from their families' drug-trafficking. Saachio, Del Pierro, and Verase, the muscle of the group, were very successful within the family. As men of honor in the family, their new postings chosen for them would be within the walls of the church. Outsiders considered the Vatican infallible so no one questioned it or the banking system. Saachio was intelligent, a born leader, and he wanted no interruption from the outside world. The family and the cardinals of the Calabria would support him. Many profited from the alliance and the three cousins had become high-ranking members of the Roman Catholic Church. It was now up to Del Pierro to retrieve the diary that had been given to Luci de Foix's family. If he didn't get his hands on that diary, the secrets within the journal would lead to the destruction of the *Administratia* and his aspirations as Pope.

The *fabrica* who worked in the Vatican were determined to rid themselves of the Pope. Cardinal Angelo Giovanni, an influential power broker in his own right and a veteran diplomat who had served under the late Pope John Paul, led the *fabrica*. Saachio had thought he would be next in line to be pope, but he'd miscalculated. The *fabrica* wing felt they were the rightful owners of the Vatican. Saachio needed the diary to find the codex to support his claim as the rightful person to remove the pope.

Saachio knew Fedrico was the one who could retrieve Esclarmonde's diary in the United States. But something had gone wrong. Fedrico had died and the only one who still survived was his cousin, Del Pierro. Saachio had little faith in him, but he had enlisted other people in motion to retrieve the diary.

Many people he knew in the academic world suspected the treasure of the Cathars was the Holy Grail from Montsegur. It was difficult to prove since the Roman Church, specifically Folques, had destroyed most of the Cathar writings. However, in the vaults of the Vatican, Saachio had made a great discovery: a note written by Folques about Esclarmonde and her diary. This discovery was so much more than most people suspected. Saachio had to have that diary. The 'Ndrangheta would expect it of him.

The Empress

We are not entitled to deprive heretics of the life, which God has given
them, simply because we believe them to be in the clutches of Satan ...
Those who are our enemies on
Earth may be our superiors in heaven.
~ Waso, bishop of Liege, 1045

On the way to the airport, Luci spotted the post office she had mailed the diary to. Inside, she retrieved part of Esclarmonde's diary and shredded the last part so no one could trace her.

Luci arrived at the airport in Edinburgh and went to the window to pick up her ticket for France. She had dropped off her rental car about an hour before and had time for a quick bite in a Scottish pub. She would go immediately to the library to begin her research and bring back the information requested by the college's benefactor.

After ordering food, Luci phoned Janet to let her know she would be arriving in France.

"Luci, where are you right now?" Janet demanded.

"You sound concerned, Janet. You wanted me to go to France. I'm close to finding out more information on Folques, the traveling troubadour and how he ended up in the Catholic Church. I needed more background information regarding the troubadours of Languedoc."

"I have been concerned. Just wasn't sure you were capable of making the flight. Given all the time we've spent working together, I'm proud you were able to get into the field and do research outside your office. Look at what you have accomplished."

"Thanks, Janet. I do want to be here, and I know this will help my class and gain the bucks for our department. By the way, did you find a substitute for my class?"

"Yes, but the students are not as excited about learning from him as they are with you."

"Wow, a compliment. I might have to leave more often," Luci said. Luci did not trust Janet. At every possible moment, Janet was telling her she needed counseling, and was always trying to undermine her confidence and self-esteem.

On the rare occasions Janet *was* at the college, it was because the president of the college was asking for her, or an award was being bestowed upon her. Not because of her work, but because of the people who worked in the department. The rest of the time, who knew where she was? *I certainly never have known.*

"Again, where are you now?"

"At Edinburgh airport. I flew to Scotland to get some background information on a lost instrument used by the troubadours. It was a dead end here, but I think I have picked up a trail that will lead me to it in France," she said, purposely not telling Janet about the *pax tablet* and the music box. "I'm at the airport, leaving for Paris as we speak."

"You should have gone to France first. That's where modern European literature originates in Occitan. That's what I told you to do," Janet snarled. "The school isn't paying you to jaunt around the country."

Back to being the bitch. "I know and I am now on my way. I'll call you when I get set up in a hotel," she said, then hung up the phone.

Picking up her sandwich, she opened the last half of the diary and carefully read the pages that applied to the Major Arcana – the secret. She saw part of the *pax tablet* inscribed in the book on the card of the Chariot and knew she was on the right path.

Sitting down, Luci pulled out the information she had gleaned from the Internet regarding the troubadours who were composers and performers of Old Occitan lyric poetry during the Middle Ages. Troubadours praised high ideals, promoting a spirit of equality based on common virtue, and they disdained discrimination based on blood or wealth. They were responsible for a great flowering of creativity and were supported by the royal families in France. On the Empress card, there was a beautiful woman shown facing forward on her throne – the traditional position of power. On the left, was a shield with a phoenix, which represented hope and resurrection. Woman troubadours, as well as men, were welcomed in the château throughout the country of Occitan.

Luci's mind drifted off as she imagined living in Occitan. She remembered a poem, *The Lives of the Troubadours,* written by Vidal, an old but feisty Druid, who had wandered from Palestine to Ireland. He was shrunken by age and bent from the many disappointments in his life, but his watery blue eyes still dazzled. He had been present at the dawn of chivalry and was rumored to have learned magical secrets from Merlin himself.

Luci believed his magic came from his great mind and the love of peace he held so dearly. She imagined Vidal being lifted by a burly knight to his feet. With great impatience, he waved them off, sadly watching the crowd of his fellow men, knowing this would be his last performance. A viol player strummed a melancholic chord. Vidal sang in a husky contra tenor voice:

Sir, had I goodly steed,
Soon would my enemies for mercy plead;
For even when they hear of men my name,
They fear me more than you doth fear hawk's greed;
Nor prize their life a do it, so fierce of deed,
So stern they know me, and so great my fame.

When donned my glitt'ring steel-lined coat of mail,
And girt my sword, his gift that cannot fail,
Whither I go, the earth doth shake with fear;
No foes I meet that do not fore me pale,
And yield me place; nought doth their pride avail,
So great their terror when my step they hear.

Great joy have I to greet the season bright,
And joy to greet the blessed summer days,
And joy when birds do carol songs of praise,
And joy to mark the woods with flowers delight,
And joy at all whereas to joy were meet,
And joy unending at the pleasance sweet,
That yonder in my joy I think so gay,
There where in joy my soul and sense remain.

'Tis love that keeps me in such dear delight,
'Tis love's clear fire that keeps my breast ablaze,
'Tis love that can my sinking courage raise,
Even for love am I in grievous plight;
With tender thoughts love makes my heart to beat,

And o'er my every wish has rule complete –
Virtue I cherish since began his reign,
And to do deeds of love am ever fain.

Luci couldn't remember any more of the man or his life. He was a true Renaissance man, powerful and passionate in his prose. A man she would have loved to have met.

The Roman Church despised him and all troubadours. Actually, they'd hated them as much as the Cathars. Luci doubted this was a coincidence. The troubadours wandered like gypsies, keeping everyday people informed of love and truth. Even Folques – or as he was later known, Folquet de Marselha, Archbishop of Toulouse – had started out as a troubadour in his early years. He was guilty of the torture of Guilhelm and the deaths of so many. Why? Was it because he wanted the treasure for himself or because Esclarmonde spurned him?

The Chariot

We can only be said to be alive in those moments when our hearts are conscious of our treasures.
~ Thornton Wilder

Air France had great accommodation. The seats turned into beds and the food was incredible. She fell asleep for what seemed like minutes when she was woken by the attendant announcing their arrival. She could feel the thrust of the airplane's engines as they descended and touched the runway.

The flight attendant's voice came over the intercom. "Welcome to Paris Charles de Gaulle. We have now landed in Paris. Please wait until the plane has come to a complete standstill before reaching for your luggage in the overhead bins."

Having looked at the guide in the pockets of the airplane seats, Luci knew that Paul Andreu designed the airport. It seemed to her like it was built in the image of an octopus and consisted of a circular central part dedicated to ensure comfort for travelers.

She collected her suitcase and walked into the middle of the building. It held a vast skylight in its center. Each floor was dedicated to a single function. The first was reserved for technical purposes, the second contained shops and restaurants, which was where Luci headed. In the beauty salon, she had the beautician cut her hair and change the color from blonde to a sophisticated red.

"Are you sure, mademoiselle, that you want to do this?" the beautician asked after examining Luci's hair.

"Yes, I need a new look. I want my hair to look like the picture that is in this *Mademoiselle Magazine*. I think it will be a perfect look for me."

† † †

The beautician just shook her head at the crazy American and did her job, and said, "If the mademoiselle wants a better look, you really should change to a smaller purse. Carrying around that big bag is certainly an 'Ugly American' idea of chic."

Embarrassed, Luci walked out of the salon, and headed for the Armani store where she purchased several outfits that would blend with the Parisian culture. Exiting Armani, she spotted Chanel and bought a beautiful black dress that fit like a glove and enhanced all the right body parts.

Her next stop was to locate a map of Paris and pinpoint the Bibliotheque du Roi, where the first tarot cards were displayed.

She might not be a detective or well-versed in whatever was going on, but she was a survivor. Slipping into a restaurant at the airport, she headed to the woman's lounge with her purchases to change her clothes. Unbuttoning her jeans, she found a crumpled napkin from the hotel she stayed at by Yale University. It had some writing that was a bit too blurry without her glasses. She could see that it was from Nick de Foix and he had signed it. He must have put the note in her jeans that night at dinner. She stuffed the letter back into her front pocket to read when she found her hotel. She was in a hurry to get to a place with WiFi connection and find out the link between the tarot, the Cathars, and the treasure that everyone wanted to get their hands on. Leaving the lounge, she headed for the third floor. There she found access to a taxi.

Hailing the driver, Luci spotted Max. "Shit, he just doesn't go away." How in the hell could he keep following her?

Calmly, she stepped into the taxi at the front of the queue and gave directions to the driver to head for Hotel le Bellechasse in Paris. It was near the Bibliotheque Nationale de France, in Saint Germain in the heart of Paris, just a few steps from the Musée d'Orsay.

Changing her mind, Luci said, "Pull over." She thought it best to change hotels.

She handed him the money for the fare. Stepping out of the cab with her suitcase, she walked quickly toward the Eiffel Tower. She wanted to make sure no one had followed her. She spotted one of the city's fanciest designer hotels. She'd heard it was the creation of couturier Christian Lacroix. A stay there was like wandering into a psychedelic garden. Each guest room was different, in a pastiche of colors with baroque overtones – something Luci adored. They even had a bath with a fiberglass skylight and, best of all, room service. She needed a home base, a place to think to try to put the mystery of the past and present together.

"Sir, do you have a room that I might stay in for a few weeks?" Luci asked in the best high school French she could muster. If only her teacher, Ms Barros, could see her now, she would be so proud.

"But of course, madam."

Luci started to hand him her credit card, but thought better of it. She had watched enough *Criminal Intent* episodes to know that Max could track her down that way so she pulled out enough cash to last her for a week. Good thing her grandparents had left her a sizable amount of money when they passed away. No one knew that she had access to it in the Isle of Mann except for her.

Jacques, the hotel keeper, handed her a key. She left, pulling her luggage behind her.

It didn't hurt that the hotel was air-conditioned and, God bless, had WiFi access. She felt she was safe enough away from Max for the time being. Things were becoming clearer than in the beginning. She knew there was a treasure and she had many clues to help to find it. What was it? That was still a mystery. She was exhausted, but decided to text Janet to let her know she was now in Paris and would be working on the history of the troubadours in the 1100s. But she didn't let her know where she was staying.

Yawning, Luci stretched out on her bed, pulled the Marseilles deck out of her purse, and began flipping the tarot cards over. She'd read in some book that you were supposed to pick the tarot cards up and turn them over from right to left, shuffle them, then divide them into three stacks. She picked up one stack and began laying the Major Arcana cards down on her bed. *Weird.* She must not have shuffled them enough because she ended up with the whole Arcana in one stack.

She picked up one card after another, laid them back on her bed, and noticed something in the Tarot of Marseilles. The Chariot, the number seven card meaning humanity and spiritual wisdom or vanity and pride, was at the top. At the bottom of the card, horses were pulling in two different directions, with the wheels pulling the opposite way. Between the horses was the insignia of the Viscomte of Toulouse – VT – Simon IV de Montfort l'Amaury, who had been disinherited from his uncle's estates in Leicester, England, and had needed the crusade to take back the wealth and position that had been taken from him. He'd made it his mission to support Pope Innocent III and kill the families of Occitan. By doing so, the pope would grant him all of those families' land.

Opening her luggage, Luci retrieved the book written by AE Waite that she had purchased just before leaving Monterey. She looked in the index and opened to the page that explained the history of the Empress. This card represented the ultimate medieval woman. Some believed the card stood for Corba, who'd killed herself rather than be taken by the Teutonic Knights and tortured to reveal the location of the treasure.

Luci called the concierge and, pulling out her rail guide, asked, "What is the easiest way to get to the Bibliotheque?"

The concierge explained that it was not far and she could walk from the hotel or they would provide a car to take her there.

"Thank you. I think I'll walk," she said, hanging up the phone.

Sitting on the bed, Luci read that the Bibliotheque was the repository of all that was published in France. The Bibliotheque Nationale de France traced its origin to the royal library founded at the Louvre by Charles V in 1368. It'd expanded under Louis XIV, opened to the public in 1692, and had grown since. The collection had swelled to over three hundred thousand volumes. During the French Revolution, people had destroyed the private libraries of aristocrats and clergy. In September 1792, the Assembly of France declared the Bibliotheque du Roi to be national property and the institution was renamed the Bibliotheque Nationale. After four centuries of control by the Crown, this library was now the property of the French people.

She noticed that the Bibliotheque du Roi housed seventeen tarot cards which had been drawn and illuminated on lambskin by Charles Gringonneur in 1393 for Charles VI of France. The cards were stunning. The figures had a background of gold and were decorated with a silver border, but, unlike the other tarot decks, these cards had no inscription and no numbers. Definitely different from the tarot cards she had purchased over the Internet.

She knew the Trump Major, the Fool, the Emperor, the Pope, Popess, the Lover, and the Tower were at the museum. According to Esclarmonde's diary, there were clues on the cards that would help her locate the Cathar codex.

Luci's stomach began to make uncontrollable gurgling noises. "I ordered room service an hour ago. Where are they?" Luci wondered aloud.

She got up from the bed and went over to the phone to check on her order when there was a knock on the door. Famished, she threw open the door and, there, in the middle of the hallway, looking gorgeous but angry, was Max.

Without being invited, he pushed the hotel door open and walked in, grabbing Luci's wrist.

"Let go, Max, or you'll regret it."

"If you think that hurts, wait until you see some of the people who have been killed chasing the treasure you're after. You think the people who murdered them are only going to grab your wrist to find out what you know?"

Luci moved to the bed and sat down, a little wary of his tirade.

"You make my job complicated and difficult," he continued. "There are things you don't know, things you don't understand, especially about the people who want the artefact. Either you're going to have to trust me, or I walk out this door. However, you had better make up your mind soon."

There was another knock. Max got up, looked through the peephole, then slowly opened it. This time it was the food. He motioned for the waiter to enter. "Do you always eat for three?" he asked Luci.

Shrugging, she had the waiter place the food on the table near the flat screen. After the waiter had arranged the plates, utensils, and bottle of wine on the table, she signed the check, and he left. Turning to Max, she said, "If we are going to start with trust, who are you really?"

"Fair enough. I am an agent for the Vatican. Since you received Esclarmonde's diary from the trust, certain members of the Vatican are very interested in the Cathar codex. The pope assigned me to protect you. You are one of the last relatives of Esclarmonde d'Alion."

"How do I know you're telling the truth?"

"You can never be sure about anyone, can you, Luci?"

"I would like to think I could trust someone sent to protect me."

"One, how naïve," Max said. "Two, your education was paid for so you could find the lost treasure of your ancestors. The codex is what the Monsignor Saachio covets and why he is after you. The Solomon treasure is just a bonus. After it is found, you're worthless to them," he said with venom.

"I'm not in a perfect position, am I?" Luci said, concerned.

"No, but if we work together and find what was secreted out of Montsegur two days before the fall, we would hold the key to your safety."

He mentioned the word *key*. Luci was not about to tell him about the key *she* had found. "Again, you say *we*, but that's not really true. Once you use me to find the treasure, what's to stop you from killing me?"

"I'd like to believe we've come to trust each other more than that, Luci," he said with a grin.

Anxious, Luci felt sure, at this moment, she could not trust anyone. She would not tell Max about the *pax tablet*, the lettering, or the music box. "How did you get involved in all of this, Max?"

"What we need to do is concentrate on finding the trail left by the tarot cards and the clues inside the book by Esclarmonde d'Alion," he said, ignoring her question.

"Are you sure it isn't the Grail? It seems everyone has a theory about the Grail and who it belongs to," she said.

"No," Max said with exasperation. Sitting at the table, he grabbed the salad and began to eat. "Would you care for a glass of wine?" he said, smiling between clenched teeth.

"Yes, thank you Max." For a while, they sat and ate in silence. Luci looked sadly over at Max, knowing the answer, but she had to ask him. "Do you know if my parents' and grandparents' deaths were an accident?"

Looking chagrined, he turned away. "I'm sorry, Luci, but the truth is, your parents and grandparents were murdered by the people who are after you and the key you hold."

Even though she knew this, she still didn't want to believe it. But this was what she had trained for all those years – to get revenge. She felt the blood drain from her face and began to breathe slowly. Quickly, she threw her fork onto the table, then raced to the bathroom. Leaning over the toilet bowl, she threw up everything she had just eaten. When there was nothing left, she sat on the tile floor and cried.

"Luci, let me explain to you what is going on." Max said through the closed door. "Luci please let me in," he pleaded. He didn't want to have to kick down the door if she started hyperventilating. He heard the shower and Luci getting into it.

"I'm sorry, Luci. Please let me be there for you." He heard the water shut off, and Luci came out the door with a towel wrapped around her.

She was shaking, and those big blue eyes of hers captured his heart. He opened his arms, and she went into them, quietly sobbing.

A deck of cards, a book, people watching her for years and paying for her education … What was happening? She didn't understand. Was any of this real? Who was doing this to her?

She looked up into Max's face, reached up, and touched her lips to his in gratitude.

He froze and let out an expletive. "Luci." Confusion and shock played across his features. He stepped between her thighs and pulled her to the edge of the bed and laid her down gently on her back. She began to unbutton his shirt as he took her towel, slowly unwrapping it from around her body. She wiggled her hips experimentally and he sucked in a sharp breath. "Please keep going, Max." Her arms wound around his neck and his lips caused an avalanche of delicious tremors inside her and made her heart speed up until she could hear it pounding in her ears.

He let out a groan and began to move slowly. His body shook and she knew he was holding on to his control. The foreign feeling of being filled entirely by Max turned into unthinkable pleasure. His slow possession of her was driving her crazy and she wanted more. She began to move, meeting his slow thrusts, silently begging for more.

"Next time, I'll take things slow, I promise."

She clung to him, not wanting to let go and very much wanting more.

"I'm here for you, Luci. I have been from the moment I saw you."

Finding her voice, she whispered, "Why in the hell did we wait so long to do that?"

Max grunted. "Because I'm a fool."

She pursed her lips, and attempted to swallow a smile. "I'm not going to argue with you there."

"We shouldn't have done this, it complicates everything." Max dressed and walked out of the room, leaving Luci staring after him. She ran to the door to call him back, but stopped herself. She kept hoping that he would explain what his connection was to her, and what the tarot cards meant. She wanted to trust him, but until she knew the answers to those questions, she couldn't.

Her shoulders sagging, she walked back to the hotel bed and made plans to visit the library on her own. She couldn't sleep. She thought of Max and wondered what he was doing. She sat and watched as the sun came up. Tired, she quietly dressed and walked out her hotel room, hating all the turmoil Max had caused inside her.

† † †

Max watched her leave the hotel room. He had just gotten off the phone with the Vatican.

Joker

The fates lead him who will; him who won't they drag.
~ Roman Quote

Downstairs in the hotel restaurant, she ate her breakfast and drank several cups of coffee. Getting up, she paid the cashier, then walked to the Bibliotheque. *I know I will find clues from the original painter of the tarot deck of cards, Charles Gringonneur,* she thought. There were no numbers or inscriptions on the cards he'd designed, which made it difficult to interpret them. These were the oldest copies of the originals that Gringonneur had painted on lambskin. Maybe one of these cards was a card that Guilhelm had held before he died.

After reading an excerpt from Esclarmonde's diary, Luci began to search the row of tarot cards. She knew the Trumps Major contained seventy-eight cards, twenty-two of which would play an important part in discovering the whereabouts of Mary Magdelene's lost scripture and possibly the location of Solomon's treasure. She pulled out her copy of the diary to see if she could spot any details that could lead them on the right path.

Looking closely at the Joker, she knew this was one of the most important cards. The Joker meant that a person had come full circle, but in the Marseilles deck it said a Cathar High Priestess in disguise. Luci was beginning to understand the cards that helped in the revelation of secrets and hidden truths, the more she discovered the closer she was to come full circle.

She gazed at the Star. It was the seventeenth card in the deck. On the card, a Cathar woman was pouring the secrets of the Cathars into the ground to revive the soil for a later time, according to the diary. Birds were sitting on trees. This meant that when nurtured, the trees would bear fruit that would spread the word of the Holy Ghost. The seven stars on the card represented the celestial bodies one passed through to reach God.

The Moon, card number eighteen, represented the fighting that had gone on in Toulouse by the Dominicans and Franciscans over the death of the Cathars. The card was represented by dogs (the Dominicans), with a wolf (the Franciscans) just beneath the fighting dogs. And under the dogs was a crayfish, which was the symbol of the Cathars in hiding. There were a sun and moon eclipses. The moon was a time of rest for the Cathars before dying, and the sun represented purification.

Should she drive to Toulouse? Was that where the cards were pointing? It was where Simon de Montfort began killing the Cathars for the pope and where they'd buried him. Maybe there were clues at his burial site.

Caught up in the beauty of the artwork on the cards, she saw a rock on the tarot. It got her thinking. The Philosopher's Stone was a part of an alchemical society that had gone deep underground, like the tarot cards. Was it real, as well?

She remembered an early-twentieth-century Frenchman whose pseudonym was Fulcanelli – an alchemist and esoteric author whose identity was still unknown. He'd written a best-selling book titled, *Le Mystere des Cathedrales*. It explained how the cathedrals of Europe were coded with messages, again not unlike the tarot cards that pointed to lost knowledge and hermeticism.

The hermetic writings had been translated into books with instructions on how to follow along with the magicians' paths. It was really the magicians' – or alchemists' – role to bridge the gap between heaven and earth. In essence, the Magician tarot card was the Christian Magus. He translated the connection between angels and demons.

Looking closely at the Magician card, Luci noticed he was raising his wand to call to the spirits of heaven. Around him were the four elements: earth, air, water, and fire. He was holding the wand in his left hand.

I wonder what the significance of that is? Is the wand supposed to represent the king? But looking at how the Magician had snatched it and held it up to the observer, it seemed as if he was in charge. Not unlike the bishop's staff with his claim to divine right.

Maybe that was why the Cathars had hated Bishop Folques. He had become a traitor to his home and to the citizens of Toulouse. The count had been one of the strongest opponents of the war.

Accompanied by Raymond VI of Toulouse, they'd left their home-land and ridden to Rome to complain of the abuses by Bishop Folques. Raymond spoke of Folques more like the anti-Christ than one of Christ's ambassadors.

Esclarmonde's diary explained that the Bishop tarot card was in reality, Bishop Folques. All the information from the cards was telling her to start her journey in Toulouse. Folques, de Montfort, and the Knights Templar constructed most of the cathedrals with hidden meanings. They were not only decorative, but informative – biblical storytelling in stone.

Looking at the Moon card, Luci saw the towers of Toulouse. Along the top of the wall were the Zodiac symbols, mathematical riddles, and geometric mazes right out of alchemical texts of the time.

"Shit." Out of the corner of her eye, she spotted Max coming toward her. She turned to walk away.

"Luci, hear me out. I've been researching the church and the two factions that are warring against each other in the Vatican and possibly why someone is after you. Can we take a walk and let me explain the things I've learned?"

The Hermit

A thankful person is thankful under all circumstances.
~ Baha' u llah

Luci and Max walked along Eleventh and Twelfth Arrondisse-ments by the Opera Bastille toward a restaurant that Max was familiar with, Au Trou Gascon. Max knew the chef's, Alan Dut-ournier, reputation for authentic cuisine. Max also knew about Alan's impressive cave, containing several little-known wines, along with a fabulous collection of Armagnacs, foie gras, and Gascony-cured ham. Max had eaten there once before and knew that they'd need a reservation. Feeling lucky with Luci beside him, he led her into the restaurant and the maître d' graciously found them a table.

They sat, looking at one another across the table. Max suggested a roast shoulder of milk-fed Pyrenees lamb with carrot flan, sautéed scallops with pumpkin, and a casserole made with duck, pork, lamb, and sausage for the main course. Their conversation was light, but Max pulled out the Hermit card. He wanted to explain his association to the Vatican, as well as to her and her ancestry.

"I was born in Italy, but raised in Washington DC, where I studied. Later I moved and received my law degree from Cambridge. I joined the army to serve my country in Afghanistan. Trained by the military as a sharpshooter, I rose in rank to become a lieutenant colonel. After my service ended, the Vatican recruited me because of my in-depth knowledge of languages. I'm fluent in French, Occitan, and Farsi. I met you at Monterey State University, California. I was there to learn Swahili. But the Vatican wanted me to watch out for you as well. I was leaving the library when I witnessed what happened to the monk. I ran toward the construction site and saw you being loaded onto the ambulance."

"Why are you so involved, Max?" Luci asked between bites of food.

Max sighed. "My family's history stretches back to a civilization developed at the beginning of the millennium. One of my relatives was a very famous hermit in the third Crusade. His name was Joachim of Flora and he possessed the gift of prophecy. Following the model of the monasteries of Mount Athos, Lebanon, and the Sinai, Joachim established convents in the mountains of Calabria, along with the straits of Messina, and on the Lipari Islands off Sicily. Among his contemporaries, he was the best author of a commentary on the Epistle of Saint John. This is also why I came to the attention of the Vatican.

"One year, Richard the Lionheart sought out my ancestor and begged him to explain chapter twelve of the epistle. Joachim hesitated, knowing that what he was about to say was heresy, but the king pleaded, and my ancestor felt it was his duty to inform the man of all that he knew.

"Joachim told the king of the woman dressed as the sun with a moon under her feet and a crown of twelve stars on her head, which represented the church. The large red snake with seven heads and seven diadems was the devil. The seven heads were the seven great persecutors of the Gospel: Herod, Nero, Constantine – who emptied the treasury of the Church of Rome – Mohammed, Melsemut, Saladin, and the anti-Christ. The first five are dead. Saladin lives and uses his power. The anti-Christ will come soon. Saladin still triumphs, but one day he will lose Jerusalem and the Holy Land."

"When will this take place, Hermit?" asked Richard the Lion-heart.

"Seven years after taking Jerusalem."

"So, have we come too early?"

"*Your coming was necessary, King. God will give you victory over your enemies and will make your name glorious. Regarding the anti-Christ, one day he will come among us and will sit on the throne of Peter.*"

"That's why I'm here. The pope believes that the anti-Christ is near. I wanted to explain how important the church and I feel you are and that my intentions are to help you find the clues before Cardinal Saachio does. He wants to use it to hurt the pope. Saachio has stolen millions of dollars and has hurt many people throughout the years, including your family. Please believe me."

"One day the lines will blur and to whom will you owe your allegiance? To me?"

The Fool

The greatest wealth is health.
~ Virgil

"Let's look for the first card and work our way to the end of the seventeen cards listed here, Max." Luci could hardly contain her excitement about continuing the search with his help, but she still had her misgivings.

He beckoned her to look at the next card. It was the Emperor. He held the magnifying glass out for her to take a closer look. "Can you get any information about the Emperor in this case?"

"Well," Luci said thoughtfully, "the Emperor is facing sideways, a sign that he has been removed from power. Do you remember the pope and Emperor Frederick of Germany? Fredrick lived during the Albigensian War and they made him a ward of Pope Innocent III when Fredrick's father died. When Frederick came of age, the pope and Emperor Frederick ended up hating one another. In essence, the card is showing the Emperor's disdain for the pope. Next to the king, is a shield and a pillar meaning worldly power, authority, or war-making tendencies." Looking more closely, she noticed a phoenix, which depicts a messenger from heaven.

"In history, the two pillars at the Temple of Solomon are said to uphold the world. People believe that one stands for the pope, the other for the emperor," she continued. "The spiritual world belongs to the pope and the earthly world belongs to the Holy Roman Emperor who receives his power from Caesar. The lines of authority blurred as the pope and his staff became more involved in the material world, the emperor's world.

"In the 1300s, Pope Boniface VIII changed the papal crown to the triple tiara. He declared he was the highest of priests and emperor over all emperors. The emperor was still strong in the German states," Luci told him. "The Teutonic Knights were the army of the king. In other areas like Languedoc, families and noble lords ruled the land during the Albigensian Crusade. The most powerful leader was Count Raimond of Toulouse, father of Esclarmonde d'Alion, and a friend of the Knights Templar and the Cathars.

"If you look closely, right here, Max –" He came closer and their bodies touched. Luci's breath hitched as she gazed at him. His crystal blue eyes darkened with passion and a hint of something untamed. She shivered as a strange combination of fear, excitement, and a deep longing she had never felt before for Max – and forgot what she was about to say.

"And ..." Max prompted her with a grin.

Disconcerted she continued, "In the Tarot of Marseilles, the Emperor's shield could be a statement of political loyalty in direct opposition to the pope and the king. Could this card mean Raimond held the authority to rule Toulouse, and that the Emperor card is actually Raimond and not Frederick?"

Max leaned over and picked up the tarot dictionary of meanings. He drew closer to Luci and whispered softly, "Because he faces sideways, it could also mean his destruction."

Luci felt hot and distracted. She reached into her purse for a copy of the Marseilles deck and laid out the Emperor and Pope cards. "The Emperor has his back to the Pope. Could it be that this was a warning to the people of Occitan? That Raimond was about to go to war with the pope?"

"Possibly, but it could also mean that Raimond was wily enough to show two faces, one submitting to the church while, in fact, opposing its authority." Max got even closer to the card and put his hand on Luci's.

Unnerved, she swallowed. "I believe this card shows Raimond's opposition to authority and his sympathy to the Cathars." She picked up the next card and looked into Max's steely blue eyes.

"Luci, the cards are playing out the same way today. Saachio is showing two faces, one as the President of the Banco de Ambrosia and to the pope, and another to the 'Ndrangheta. Now let's go to your room and you teach me more about the tarot cards."

She smiled, but teaching was the farthest thing from her mind. Readily, she took Max's hand and, almost at a run, left the restaurant.

† † †

Standing just around the corner of the restaurant was Dr Janet Gaetos looking at Luci with disgust.

The Sun

Among Politicians the esteem of religion is profitable;
the principles of it are troublesome.
~ Benjamin Whichcote

"The Sun card also shows how relative peace was achieved when Raymond VII's daughter, Jeanne, and Alphonse were engaged to be married. This could also represent my quest. A naked baby is riding a white horse at the forefront of the card, wearing a crown of flowers. Are we witnessing the unveiling of something important? Behind the horse is a large gray brick wall that serves as a planter with sunflowers. Behind it is a cloudless blue sky, dominated by the sun. Many things are going on." *Like in my own life*, Luci thought. "The sun indicates the universe is working in my favor." *Good to know.* "The white horse represents being taken along on my journey with less effort." *Could this be with the help of Max?* "The baby is representative of a new phase in my life. The sun illustrates a higher mind. Built in the knowledge of a higher purpose in life with intuition on how to maximize it to its fullest potential."

Things were coming to a head, Luci could feel it. She knew she was on the right path and she needed Max, just like Jean and Alphonse had needed each other.

† † †

Taking her phone out of her coat pocket, Janet quickly dialed a man she had dated and who was working for Saachio. "I need your help now. Take the next flight to France and I will meet you at the Hotel Mercure Chartres. I think we might have to arrange another accident."

"This will cost you, Janet. I will meet you at noon where we can negotiate terms at that time."

"Luci seems to be a little too cozy with Max, which could present us with a problem. We need to find out who this guy is."

"Janet, I'm looking forward to our meeting," he sneered.

"Cardinal Saachio is the one giving the directions and will pay you handsomely. I need Luci to listen to me and I don't want anyone interfering, I have been in contact with the Vatican. I've always taken care of you and given you what you needed, haven't I? When this is all done, you and I will have more money than you can imagine, and more time to spend together, Tony."

"I understand."

"Before we do anything, let's find out what Max's stake is in all of this. Maybe we buy him off."

"We need to be careful, Janet. Not all things are as they seem," Tony said with mock sincerity.

Esclarmonde's Diary

September, 1209
I rode swiftly to my father, the Comte de Foix's court. He was directing the siege of Mirepoix's troops. The fighting was fierce and reinforcements sent by the pope himself came from the Roman knights. The military orders were "true orders" of the Roman Church, governed by regulations similar to those governing monks. Later, I found out that in payment for the murder of so many, the pope gave many sacred relics, including Solomon's seal, to anyone who killed a Cathar. To differentiate themselves from the Knights Templar who were sympathetic to the Cathars, the Roman knights wore a black cross across their robes. The knights were fierce and the simple people of Mirepoix were no match.

Loup and I fought alongside our father. To the left, I spotted a man on a bay horse readying his bow. He let it fly. I could do nothing to stop the arrow from piercing my father's armor. I had no fear of man, but many of the lords and ladies who had defended the Cathars and protected their beliefs were now alone to face the Romans. I kneeled beside my dying father and grabbed hold of him.

"Dear God, Papa, don't die," I begged him. "We need you to help us continue the fight." He was one of the last leaders of the Cathars. I didn't know how we could continue fighting these battles without him. Before my father died, his last words to Loup and me were to help guard the secrets of the Cathars to the very end.

"Everything that is good will be destroyed by the church, and all our lands will be confiscated by King Louis." With his last ounce of strength, he took hold of Loup by his hair. Blood was spewing down his chin. "You must continue the battle. The future of our lands depend upon you and your sister," he said, looking at us.

After our father's death, I developed a bond with my father's friend who was Lord of Mirepoix, Bernard d'Alion, and twenty years my senior. In a gesture of chivalry, Bernard married me to keep me safe under his protection.

The marriage was never consummated, but by marrying him, I helped safeguard a vital supply line to Montsegur after the destruction of the Mirepoix army. Montsegur had been granted to me as part of my dowry. Together, we helped keep the people in Montsegur fed and safe, while Loup continued to fight on the battlefield.

Many times, I left my husband and went back to my father's castle. I burnt all my regal clothes and jewelry. I got on my horse and left for the trackless woodland of the Capsir Mountains where I, again, met up with my brother. Clad in lightweight-mail armor specially made for my body, I helped support my brother and the champions of Occitan against the well-fortified knights.

One night, my brother came to me while I was sleeping and asked if I would stand guard while he climbed a narrow tree and lit the beacons so they might communicate to the refugees to get them safely to my husband's castle. There were still a few Cathars and Jews left in Mirepoix.

Without a word, I watched as Loup lit the beacons. In the tall oak branches, I spied crusaders making their way to my brother's encampment. Grabbing my brother's leg, I told him of the knights who were heading our way. We rushed to the side of the cliff and he pushed over one large rock that would impede their progress.

Many men dreamed of capturing me. I was once a selfish and foolish young girl, now I was a living spirit who took my oath to my father and aunt to heart. I did not believe all that Corba did. I was not a virgin, nor would I ever take the vows of a prefect. I would, however, defend my country, my family, and the rights of others to believe as they chose. My aunt had asked me to safeguard the Cathars' last codex until someone came after me to take up the fight. This, I would do.

More knights were arriving. Loup and our followers escaped. We rode back to Montsegur where Bernard d'Alion intended to break through the Roman knights' lines and end the siege at Montsegur. I knew this was a fool's journey. He would never make it back.

He told me that he had spoken with Pierre-Roger and they were about to arrange a ceasefire with the knights. "Our people are too weak to continue the fight and our defenders have been injured.

The women and children are too hungry to carry on. You need to leave with a knight I will send with you. I am giving you this opportunity to secret out the treasure of Solomon and the codex handed down to us by Mary Magdalene. You need to leave immediately."

"Please do not ask me to leave you," I begged of him.

"The time is almost here. You need to ride away."

I grabbed onto Bernard. He looked at me with sad eyes and said that he loved me. "We will meet again, my love, not in this life, but the next."

It had been a marriage of convenience. I could never love him as I loved Guilhelm. However, he had been good to me, accepted me, and I loved him in my own way.

The Lovers

Let us rise up and be thankful, for if we didn't learn a lot today, at least we learned a little, and if we didn't learn a little, at least we didn't get sick, and if we got sick, at least we didn't die; so, let us all be thankful.
~ Gautama Buddha

Luci aged 30
It was a gentle kiss, not hard, nor demanding, but the heat and thoroughness of it made Luci dizzy. Her lips parted. Her eyes softly closed. Her hands found Max's chest as her heart began to pound. She opened her eyes to see him studying her face, his eyes and his mouth so tender.

"Mmmm," she said a breath away from his lips.

Then she kissed him, soft and leisurely – a long, deep kiss that lasted until his endurance snapped. He began to trail kisses along her jaw and then down her neck. She moaned when his teeth raked over the sensitive skin just beneath her ear. He pushed her robe off her shoulders and focused his attention there. His arms tightened around her, his mouth went hot and hard, and he twisted with her in his arms so that she was lying on her back with the towel beneath her.

And there it was, rising up in her, the fire, the heat, the hunger for him that there was just no doing anything about.

"Max," she whispered when his mouth left hers to trail hot, wet kisses down the side of her neck.

His mouth found her breasts, and his teeth closed on each nipple in turn. She gasped. When his mouth left her, he rose up over her again, and she had just that split second to catch her breath, grab her sanity, and think as well as feel. She opened her eyes to find him appearing over her. His face was hidden in the shadows, but she could see the hot gleam of his eyes, the heavily muscled shoulders, the strong arms. She ached for him. Her body quaked and throbbed for him.

"Please, I need you," she begged in a quivering whisper.

"I want you more than I have ever wanted anyone in my life." His voice was hoarse and deep, his mouth unsmiling as he bent to her.

Even as she lifted her mouth for his kiss and wrapped her arms around his neck, pulling him down to her, she had that one moment of clarity in which she saw the soot-black sky and the twinkling stars out the window. She smelled the muskiness that was pure man and realized she was lying naked on a towel with the lover of her dreams – and that this night with Max was the closest she had ever gotten to paradise in her life.

He drove into her – huge, hard, and urgent – and the resulting undulating waves of passion that claimed her erased every vestige of coherent thought from her mind. Exhausted, they fell asleep in each other's arms.

The sun was coming up over the horizon.

"Luci," he whispered.

His mouth slid across her cheek, down to her neck. Her eyes opened. He kissed her on her eyes, her nose, then slid down and began to kiss and play with her nipples with his teeth. This aroused her. She thought she had been satisfied, but Max sent her onto another plane, one she had never been to before and would always remember. Aroused, she watched Max, his face, his chest, slowly moving almost to the rhythm of her breaths.

Later, Max got up to take a shower. Luci tumbled out of bed, headed directly to her laptop, and looked up the tarot card called The Lovers. The Marseilles deck referred to it as the Two Paths. The man in the middle had to choose between the matriarchal figure on his right, representing the institutional church, and the fair maiden on his left side – his heart.

It seems like this is the position I'm in. Which path do I take; the one where I go it alone, or to the one on the left – the one my heart believes? In the card, Luci noticed an angel. *I hope that angel will lead me to the true path.*

Justice

There is only one religion, though there are a hundred versions of it.
~ George Bernard Shaw

Max and Luci left the hotel after breakfast. Heading out the front door of the Hotel le Bellechasse, down the waterfront of the Seine, into the Bibliotheque du Roi, they continued their search for the Fool card and what it represented. As they were walking, Max recognized a store that one of his relatives owned, called Langue-doc.

"Let's go in and see if my great uncle still owns the store. He used to have many antiquities, mostly concerning the Cathars. He might have information to help us in our search."

Feeling a little lazy after the afternoon's activities, Luci was in a very calm and relaxed mood. "I don't need to take pills if we do this every day," she said, smiling demurely up to Max. "However, yes, I'd like to meet someone who may have information."

"My great uncle got into selling antiques, which worked well with his studies of ancient Beligirux artefacts at the university. Here's his place. Let's go in."

Luci looked through the sizeable paned-glass window into a marvelous store that had antiques of every description. Fascinated, she walked through the door only to bump into an old man who was kneeling down to fix a table from the King Louis the Fifth Era. Max caught her just before she toppled over him.

"Thanks. You seem to be getting me out of a lot of trouble lately," she said with a smile.

Max beamed back at her and, helping her up, introduced her to his uncle, Ron Visconti. "Hello, Uncle. It's been a long time since I last saw you."

"Max, if you're not the spitting image of your mother. How are Ida and Michael?"

"Fine. They live in Virginia, growing peanuts, living the good life in retirement – well, if you can call working a farm retirement."

Luci gazed at the table that she'd almost fallen over, enchanted by the exotically colored wood.

"I've always thought to retire would be boring. Who would tell the stories of the past through these beautiful pieces of furniture, glass, maps, and books?" Ron said, "I see that piece has caught your eye."

"It is quite beautiful," Luci uttered.

"During King Louis's reign, his furniture was always finely made by master craftsmen. Look closely. Do you see the branches, flowers, and seashells?"

"It's exquisite," she said. Wandering around the store, she looked for anything regarding the Cathar history – maybe a map, book … something. "Actually, that is why we stopped by. We are looking for information about the Cathars."

Max's uncle grinned at Luci. "Are you looking for a lost treasure? The Holy Grail possibly?"

"No, not really. A diary was sent to me by one of my relatives who was a Cathar. Her name was Esclarmonde."

Ron became very excited. "Do you have the diary with you?"

Taken aback, by his intensity, Luci frowned. "Of course not," she said.

"Is there a way you can get me that book? There are many people interested in it. A man contacted me not too long ago who would pay quite a bit of money for it. I can call him and we can make some arrangements."

"Sorry, I'm not interested in the money. I want to find the history behind the Cathars. What happened to them? Are there still scrolls that document their beliefs? And why were they such a threat to the Roman Church? That's what I am looking for."

Max leaned against the wall, watching Luci talk to his uncle. "I understand. I, too, have always been interested in the history." He felt his phone vibrate. "Excuse me. I need to take this call."

"Sure, Max." When Max left, Ron asked Luci, "Would you like some tea, my dear, while we wait?"

"Thank you, but no. We need to get to the museum, but Max hadn't seen you in so long, he wanted to stop by to see if you still owned the store. He also hoped that you would have some information regarding the Cathars. Oh, there you are, Max. We were beginning to wonder where you had gone for so long."

"Sorry, it was work."

"Why don't the two of you go out to Tuileries Gardens for a walk while I look around the store?" Ron suggested. "I might have something on the Cathars somewhere. I'm just not sure where I last saw it, then I'll take you to my favorite café."

"Thank you Ron," Luci said. "It would be much appreciated."

Leaving the store, she and Max walked hand-in-hand to the Tuileries Palace, which had stood on the right bank of the River Seine until 1871.

"It was destroyed in upheaval during the suppression of the Paris Commune," Max told her. "It's surrounded by the Louvre to the east, the Seine to the south, the Place de la Concorde to the west, and the Rue de Rivoli to the north."

"How large is it, Max?"

"The Tuileries Garden covers about sixty-three acres and closely follows the design laid out by the royal landscape architect, Andre Le Notre, from 1664. Look over there, Luci. You can see an unbroken vista along a central axis from the west façade. Beautiful, isn't it?"

"It's like time stood still."

They continued their stroll through the green oasis and stopped to watch the children playing in a pool, the families checking out boats, and people floating along the bank.

"Did you know that in the springtime chairs are lined up for visitors to sit and watch the blossoming of the sixty thousand bulbs?" Max asked her. "Tuileries is named for the clay soil with which Parisians make their tile."

"No I didn't. I wish we didn't have to go back to the store, it's like heaven here. But we need to get back to your uncle's place," she said looking at her watch.

"Yeah, it's getting late and I'm sure my uncle will want to close up for the evening."

† † †

Walking back to his uncle's shop, Max opened the door for Luci and they proceeded to go in. It was very quiet. Too quiet.

Max pushed Luci behind him. He had a bad feeling and trusted his intuition. Because of it, he was still breathing. They began to search out the whereabouts of his uncle. The place was eerily empty. Max headed for the back room in case Ron was downstairs and couldn't hear them.

† † †

Luci went to the left toward an alcove where she found Max's uncle. A long spiked candlestick, usually placed next to an altar in the Roman Church, had been shoved up his anus. He was still alive, but slowly bleeding out.

Luci screamed for Max. "Who could do this? Max!" she cried out.

Ron beckoned Luci to come closer. "Luci – the diary – the diary – they need it – don't – mustn't trust anyone – look behind the miniature Eiffel – card – don't trust."

"Sssh. I'll call an ambulance for you, Mr Visconti."

Max walked in and raced to his uncle's side. "Luci, call an ambulance immediately," he commanded, panicked.

Luci ran out of the room and went to Ron's desk. She found the card by the miniature Eifel Tower – The Lovers – just where Ron had said it would be. Picking up the card, she placed it in her jacket pocket and then called for an ambulance.

"I need help. I'm dying, Max, please help me."

† † †

Max leaned in closer. "What did you tell, Luci?" he asked.

Ron looked up at Max, leered at him as blood spilled out of his mouth and down his chin.

"We need to get out of here before the ambulance arrives, Luci," Max said with irritation.

"What? Your uncle needs help. We can't leave him alone."

"The people who did this will be watching. There's a back door. We can slip out of here unnoticed, but we have to move quickly."

"But, Max, how can we leave him alone?"

Grabbing Luci's arm, he pulled her toward the back entry and out into the alley, heading back to their hotel to pick up their belongings. "Move, Luci. They could be coming any minute."

Racing down the street, they heard the ambulance's siren.

Luci pulled away from Max. "How could you leave him dying? He's your uncle for God's sake."

"There was nothing we could do. Luci, do you know how to remove a candlestick out of someone's ass? I sure don't and whoever did this wants the diary. Uncle Ron probably told them we were coming back. Why don't you just give the diary to me now and I can take it to a bank and put it in a safe deposit box?"

"Forget it, Max. It stays with me. Anyway, it's already in a safe deposit box."

"Then what have you been hiding in your backpack?"

"Just bits and pieces of information I have collected so far."

"You're not doing that great a job so far. I'm sorry, that's not true. Look, I'm tired. Let's get to our room and get out of here."

They arrived at the hotel and raced up the stairs to their room. Throwing their clothes into their bags, they headed for the door to run out. The door crashed open, broken by a man who looked like a giant. He strode into the room with two other men. One was Reynaldo, the other, who was smaller, spoke to Max.

"Give us the book, Max, then you and Luci can be on your way."

"We don't have it," she said.

"Shut up, Luci." Reynaldo said.

"Okay," said Max. "We'll give you the location of the diary on one condition."

"You cannot make conditions, Max," the giant said, pointing a gun at Luci.

†††

Luci couldn't believe this was truly happening. "My God, what is going on?" Reynaldo was a friend of hers.

"Luci's right," Max argued. "We wouldn't be stupid enough to have the book on us. Let her go get the book. I'll stay right here with you until she gets back."

"Mmm, tempting, but no," he countered. "We keep her. You get the book and return it to us. Right Tony?" Reynaldo said to the man who looked like a gorilla.

"Okay, but don't hurt her. Sorry, Luci, I promise I'll bring the diary back."

Luci began to panic; she pleaded with Max not to leave her. She didn't have the diary. Luci had left it back home at her bank. Just what she had told Max only moments ago.

Max started to walk toward the door and, as everyone's eyes were on Max, Luci slid her leg down and around Tony, flipping him onto his back. Dropping down, she grabbed the gun and shot him. Max fell onto his side and, as Reynaldo started to make a grab for Luci, Max shoved him aside. Reynaldo let go of her and ran out the door. Luci began to shake, her breathing labored.

"Stop it, Luci," Max yelled. "We have to get out of here before the cops come."

Luci grabbed her purse, reached in for Clonazepam, then swallowed it. Picking up her suitcase, she stumbled. Max grabbed her holding her tightly. She felt a shudder run through her body as they fled down the back stairwell toward the rental car in the garage.

Once in the car, Luci couldn't stop shaking. To get her mind off of what had just happened, Max asked, "Where did you learn to fight like that?"

"My grandparents put me in Kung Fu classes and I competed in tournaments, including the championship tournament in Long Beach, California."

"You beat a young boy with dark hair and blue eyes in your last fight, didn't you?"

"How could you know that?" Luci asked, surprised.

"That boy was me." Max grinned. "I looked for you for years so we could have a rematch. You humiliated me. Where did you go?"

"My grandparents felt I was getting too aggressive and gave me horseback riding lessons instead. Max, why didn't you help me with those men? They were out to hurt me."

"I was going to shoot them, but you were in the way, Luci."

Luci gazed at him, clearly not believing what he just proclaimed.

"Max, I need to tell you about the Lovers' card. It points to two significant figures in the Albigensian War. This could be us, Max. It's the Lovers' card, a, and it's the card of two paths. Do we continue, knowing that our lives are in danger? Or do we stop? In the tarot card, you are the man in the middle. What do you choose, Max? I'm going on. The figure on the right, the old woman, represents the church. You are Catholic. Being with you puts me in jeopardy."

Max looked at Luci and pointed to the Lovers' card in her hand. "You see the maiden on the left of the man? She is on the side of his heart, as you are to me. Look at the angel. He is pointing to you, Luci. I stay with you. You are my heart and I will never let you go," he said softly. "We go together or neither of us goes."

"I thought you didn't know anything about tarot cards. You've got two faces showing, Max. Which one have you kept hidden from me? You promised that I could trust you. You said you told me everything. *You haven't.* You're holding something back. Pull over, I'm going alone," she ordered.

Sometimes in your life, circumstances changed or changed you. It was time she found the underlying cause of her family's murders and who'd killed them. Time she stopped being a passenger on the train of life. She was tired of people making decisions for her and of living her life vicariously through books.

Max pulled the SUV over, and Luci exited.

"Please Luci."

On the corner, she hailed a taxi and drove to the train station. Sitting in the cab, she began to sob. She was hurt. She was alone and frightened. Her eyes became blurry from the tears. Paying the taxi driver, she stepped out of the cab, walked into the station, and headed for the bathroom.

Leaning over the bathroom sink, she splashed water on her face. She didn't want to be a meek little mouse any longer. She didn't like Janet, but at least she had always been consistent – a liar, a thief of others' academic work, and a master manipulator, but Luci could use this to her advantage. She took her phone out of her purse and placed a long distance call to Janet.

†††

Janet who had been following Luci to the train station heard her phone ring. Taking it out of her coat pocket, she saw it was Luci. "Where have you been, Luci? I've been worried sick about you. There was a report of an antique dealer who was found murdered not far from the museum on the news."

"We were there, Janet. It was horrible and I just don't know who to trust any longer. Why did you send me here?"

"You know why you're there, Luci. A benefactor is interested in your findings in Languedoc. Why? What's going on?"

"People I thought were my friends, aren't. I found out that my grandparents were murdered and my parents' car crash wasn't an accident, after all. This is just too crazy. I need to come home. I can't continue to do this anymore."

"Are you giving up, Luci? Because that's what you typically do."

"How can you say that to me? It's not true and you know it. I've allowed you to take credit for my work. I never cared if my name was on a publication. You're saying this to me when I just told you everyone I know and trusted has died. Someone even just tried to kill me."

"Is he dead?"

"I don't know, Janet. We ran out of the hotel."

"Is Max with you? I know how close you've become."

"No," she said quietly – Luci didn't remember telling Janet anything about Max.

"Okay, Luci, calm down. You know I care about you. You can trust me. I'll take the next flight out to France and meet you at the Cathedral of Our Lady of Chartres. I'll call you when I land."

"All right. I'll meet you at the cathedral in the next few days." Closing her phone, Luci headed for the ticket counter.

† † †

As for Janet, she wondered what Antonio was up to.

Esclarmonde's Diary

January, 1212
The widespread revolt was happening in Occitania against the French Crown and Roman authorities. The rebellions failed and the leading local overlord, Raymond VII, the Count of Toulouse, in whose territory Montsegur fell, signed a final peace treaty with the French King, Louis IX. Raymond VII, who had rebelled and was, until then, a Cathar supporter, was forgiven by the king and the church. As a sign of peace between Raymond and the pope, Montsegur was to be destroyed, along with everyone in it.

I heard from a soldier that a Roman conclave held in Beziers in the spring of 1209 put out a call to bring down the "synagogue of Satan" at Montsegur. By Ascension Day, on the anniversary of the assassination of the Inquisitors. I watched as knights, supported by local troops forced into service, began to pour into the valley below the swamp at Montsegur. Over the next ten months, ten thousand soldiers would gather beneath the fortress, drawing closer and tightening the perimeter around Montsegur.

Pierre-Roger and the Cathars had been living within the fortress in a small terraced village just beneath the northeastern slope of the current fortress wall. Small settlements also dotted the northern face of the pog, which gently sloped downward, away from the fortress like a camel's back, and finished at yet another manned outpost know as Roc de Latour. The main southwestern approach to the fort was very steep and protected by several walls. Despite all the Roman troops, many secret footpaths were leading up to the fortress Corba had shown me as a child. I continued to send messages, troops, refugees, and provisions through the French lines – both in and out of Montsegur.

Pierre-Roger commanded the defense of Montsegur. He had a total of seventy men: eighteen battle hardened knights, six light horse riders, and three crossbow men sympathetic to the Cathars. Other troops, archers, and hired mercenaries rounded out the number of defenders at Montsegur to approximately a hundred and fifty warriors in total.

When I was not transporting supplies, I was with Aunt Corba. As the siege unfolded for the first eight months, the Roman forces painstakingly attempted to take the slopes of the mountain to powerful position trebuchets within range of the castle. Yet the hills proved to be so impregnable that, the Romans became severely demoralized by their lack of progress, and the villagers grew more hopeful.

I had left Montsegur to get more provisions but, in the dark, I watched as Gascon mountain troops climbed the northeastern tip of the hill in the middle of the night and captured the lowest point of the plateau – the Roc de la Tour. I watched as the Roman troops began to fight their way up toward the fortress, capturing positions for a trebuchet and using the resources of the plateau to construct the catapult and launch the stone missiles. Our fate was sealed. We made several counter-attacks to dislodge the crusaders, but it was too late. Heavy reinforcements had poured up through the rear part of the pog and were dug in.

On 1 March 1212, Pierre-Roger de Mirepoix emerged from the fortress and negotiated a two-day truce, at the end of which Montsegur would surrender. The mercenaries would be allowed to leave with their weapons. Any Cathar who denied their faith would be forgiven. Lords, ladies, knights, soldiers, craftsmen, and servants would be allowed to depart.

When all seemed to be lost, Aunt Corba took me to the top of the castle and gave me the instructions about the location of the treasures.

Aunt Corba told me I was their only hope to prevent these documents from falling into the hands of the Roman Church. They would destroy them and she would not chance that. "You have no choice but to leave, survive, and get the treasure to a safe place. Loup will leave with you and then head for Montserrat."

Torn at the thought of leaving my aunt, I grabbed hold of her. "You are my light. If you die, we will all be cast into the shadow of the Roman Church."

"You must leave, to carry on, and that, from that day forward, I would be known as the White Lady. You will save the treasures for future generations," Corba told me.

I grabbed hold of my aunt's hand but it was no use. I knew that Corba needed me to safeguard the treasures. I had the codex sealed in a metal cylindrical container that, if one were paying attention to the tarot cards we had sent out, it would be found one day. I prayed I would not let Corba down.

I kissed my aunt. Turning, I fled down the stairs. I could hear Corba speak to the people below her. All eyes looked up at the glorious sight. No one was watching me as I crept down the parapet to the stables. My aunt had given me the opportunity to escape.

Corba was a courageous woman. On a hilltop, I turned and watched as Aunt Corba stood and waited until she saw me far beyond the walls of the castle on my white steed with my brother, Loup and another knight headed off to Usson.

I stopped just in time to see my Aunt Corba lift her hand as if to wave a farewell, then leap over the precipice without hesitation. Some have said she assumed the form of a dove to carry the Holy Grail away from those who had persecuted the Cathars.

† † †

No body or grave of Corba's has ever been discovered, or that of the Grail.

Pope

We are no mere men. We have the place of God here on earth."
~ Pope Innocent IV

Luci aged 30
The next morning, Luci left the hotel for the Notre Dame de Chartres. She'd had no time to look closely at the card that Max's uncle had told her to retrieve. Now on the metro, she pulled it out of her pocket and studied it.

She remembered his final words to her. "Trust no one, Luci."

Reading the Lovers' card, she knew where she might find the next clue. According to what Max had told her, she could see there was a lot at stake, including the destruction of the banking side of the Vatican by The Order – an organization headed by Cardinal Saachio. It was a Roman Catholic congregation of pontifical right, made up of priests and seminarians studying for the priesthood, the priestly and religious branch of the apostolic lay movement, headed by Cardinal Saachio, a friend at one time of John Paul II. Members of the Legion took vows of obedience, chastity, and poverty. They initially made a private vow of charity, promising never to criticize their superiors. The Vatican opposed this private vow when it chartered the Legion decades ago, but that opposition disappeared after a final decision by the Vatican in 1983. Pope Benedict XVI repealed this vow in 2007, following revelations of sexual abuse.

She knew she was getting closer to the truth. It was the cylinder in the hand of Mary Magdalene in a famous painting. Mary was the one Jesus trusted the most. She was the only one who did not abandon Jesus at his crucifixion. Mary had remained steadfast by the cross to listen to the last words spoken by Jesus, and later wrote them down in her gospel found at the Nag Hammadi. When Jesus was buried, she'd stayed by the entrance of the tomb. The Cathars protected this last codex from the Romans. On the cup tarot, Mary Magdalene might be the youth who held a cup with a snake. Could this be a missing tarot card? Luci would keep this information to herself.

When she got off on the Rue Felibien, it was raining heavily. She walked, with an umbrella in hand, to the Notre Dame de Chartres Cathedral's south entrance. She wanted to make sure she covered as much of the cathedral as possible to gather information she could later use. From that distance, she caught a glimpse of the two tall towers of Our Lady of Chartres glimmering in the moonlight over the land, sometimes illuminated by lightning flashes like trees twisted by the wind. It was a safe haven. Soon, her thoughts wandered to where Janet was and why she had promised to meet her but had not yet arrived.

Notre Dame de Chartres, a twelfth-century French cathedral dedicated to the Virgin Mary, was just fifty miles from Paris. The current cathedral had been constructed between 1193 and 1250, built over a druidic temple.

Luci wondered who the Virgo Paritura was supposed to be. Could it be Mary or Esclarmonde? Climbing the stairs, she was now at the level of the sanctuary, on a large square whipped by the wind from every direction and pounded by the rain. Entering the cathedral by the southern portal, Luci was immediately plunged into a blue radiance. Yet the dark sky was casting little light. She had to believe that the stained glass windows of Chartres possessed their own illumination, strong enough on its own without needing sunlight, like an inner glow.

Luci felt she was in another world. On the floor were beautiful stones laid out like a trail that she was to follow. If the luminaries with flickering flames had been made of gold, she felt she would have arrived in Oz. The statue of Our Lady loomed out of the darkness on her pillar. Luci decided it might be prudent to spend money on a tour guide. She didn't know the cathedral and needed help.

Walking up to the guide booth, she spotted a young man dressed in a plaid jacket and bow tie. She figured this man young, eager, with his hair combed back and thick black-rimmed glasses was an academic. She felt he would know the cathedral inside and out. She paid the money required for a private tour guide, and the young man immediately began his memorized talk.

They walked to the Gallery of Kings, which had a strong vertical thrust at the base of the towers. The light of the Ile-de-France glided over the spare surfaces, penetrating the void.

"Excuse me, Timothy," Luci said. "I hate to interrupt you, but why is this cathedral named after Mary, and what did the Knights Templar have to do with the construction?"

"I can only speculate on the rumors that I have heard while working here," Timothy informed her. "After Jesus rose from the dead, he asked Joseph of Arimathea to take his mother, Mary Magdalene, and a young maid with the treasure of a seal ring. Mary kept her codex, and later, the name of God was engraved. They lived out their days here with many Knights Templar protecting them. Jesus' mother, Mary never recovered from the grief of the death of her son. When she passed, the Knights built a cathedral over a chapel. After many years, the cathedral was nearly

destroyed. The knights rebuilt the cathedral, and Pierre de Mon-
treuil, another knight, succeeded in finishing it in 1243. At that
time, the Roman knights had already attacked Montsegur. Three
Cathars made their escape out of Montsegur with a treasure. That
is the last that most of us know about what happened during that
time. Many say they came here and secreted the cache within the
cathedral. Many also believe that Esclarmonde was pregnant and
she is the one this cathedral is dedicated to. The Cathedral is also
referred to as the Black Madonna."

Luci didn't know about that piece of information and tucked it
into the back of her mind. Could Mary Magdalene be the one who
so many speculate carried the Merovingian bloodline? Or maybe
it was Esclarmonde who carried a child as a ruse to confuse the
church.

"On your left, look at the inscription written on this plaque on
the wall. Not only is Chartres Cathedral one of the greatest
achievements in the history of architecture, but Chartre's portal
sculpture also remains intact, and it's beautifully preserved. The
stained glass windows are all original. They were all crafted by the
Knights Templar.

"Just down the hall, on your left is a silver plaque, which states
that the Chartres Cathedral acquired the *Sancta Camisa,* believed to
be the tunic worn by the Blessed Virgin Mary at the time of Christ's
birth. According to legend, the tunic was given to the cathedral by
Charlemagne. He received it as a gift from Emperor Constantine
VI during a crusade to Jerusalem. Because of its importance to the
Catholic Church, the tunic has been the Marian pilgrimage center
of the faithful," Timothy stated.

"What an incredible history this cathedral has. Its existence is a
miracle," Luci said.

"Something you might find interesting is that there is a labyrinth
over there which has attracted pilgrims since the 1100s."

Luci followed the guide, checking out places that she might hide
for a plan she had been thinking about.

"Many of the pilgrims come to walk or crawl slowly around the
blue and white flagstones with their heads bowed in prayer,"
Timothy continued. "It is amazing to see how strong faith can be
to so many. The labyrinth is important because there are two
hundred and ninety-two stone steps, the length of a baby's gesta-

tion. All that remains of the brass plaque that formerly decorated the center of the labyrinth are the worn stubs of the rivets that held it in place. It bore a representation of the combat between Theseus and the Minotaur. There are various ideas to the meaning of the labyrinth; some consider it a simple decorative element. Still others believe that it contains Hermetic writings, and some believe that something of great importance is buried beneath the center."

"Timothy, thank you for the tour."

"I have always considered this my second home, Ms de Foix, and am happy to share my knowledge with the people who come to visit. Let me go on. I think you will find this interesting as well. During construction, Chartres was known as the House of Daedalus, equating it with the intricacy of labyrinths. In the cathedrals, the *Domus Dei*, the work of Daedalus, was by the master builder of antiquity and the designer of the original labyrinth.

"During the Merovingian and early Carolingian eras, the main focus of devotion for pilgrims was a well that is now located in the north side of Fulbert's crypt. It is the Well of the Strong Saints, into which the bodies of the various local early Christian martyrs – including saints Piat, Cheron, Modesta, and Potentianus – had been tossed. The widespread belief of Christians was that the cathedral was also the sight of a pre-Christian gypsy sect who worshipped a *Virgin who will give birth*."

Just as Janet was about to disembark from her jet she had received a phone call, demanding her presence in the countryside of Rome.

A limousine picked her up at the airport and they flew in a helicopter to an empty field where the only thing standing in the desolate area was a red barn. Exiting the aircraft, she walked with Antonio, one of Saachio's men, to the barn door. Entering through the dimly lit room, the cardinal's staff escorted her up a grain shaft elevator that had individual rooms for special guests. Entering, Janet was surprised to see her long-time friend, Reynaldo, on his knees, crying. Janet glared at Reynaldo for shooting her in her own home. "Good evening, Cardinal."

"You screwed up again, Reynaldo, Cardinal Saachio whispered maliciously. You were to befriend Luci as an old acquaintance and get her to trust you as she did when she was a child. My guards tell me that you tried to kill her and Max Dantie. I need that diary and

Luci has the diary that holds the key. I don't need murder on my hands. Now they are on their way to Chartres. Do you even know who Dantie is?"

"No, Cardinal. Father Del Pierro told me to get rid of him and to retrieve the diary from Luci by any means."

Looking frightened, Reynaldo glanced over at Janet. She would tell Saachio of her deceit, she thought.

"I'm sorry, Cardinal," Reynaldo said. "It won't happen again. We weren't prepared for Max and Luci to come back so soon. Ron worked for Del Pierro for years. We thought we could trust him, but he sent Luci and Max away before we could get there. He said that he had Esclarmonde's diary within reach. It was a ruse, we are sure of it. We also tried to get the remaining card that was entrusted to him but, even with torture, he wouldn't talk. I thought you would want me to bring the diary with the tarot card directly to you."

"Are you sure that you and Del Pierro aren't trying to get the diary and, therefore, the treasure for yourselves? I can't trust you, nor Del Pierro anymore. Please take him away Antonio. I no longer want to see his deceitful face."

"Please, no, Cardinal. I'm sorry. It won't happen again. Call Father Del Pierro. He will vouch for me. I'm a loyal servant to him and to you."

"No, Reynaldo, you are immoral along with Del Pierro, and he will be dealt with as well. We don't need that kind of corruption in our new world church. Take him away."

Tony grabbed Reynaldo by his arm and pulled him into the next room. Janet looked at Reynaldo, who had been beaten savagely by Saachio's men. His face was bruised and bleeding. She felt no emotion as the men took him into another room and closed the door.

Immediately, she could hear him scream. A man with leather gloves walked past her and opened the door. Peering in, she could see Reynaldo stretched out. In one corner lay a heavy wagon wheel encased in iron. This was an ancient way to torture someone, one of Saachio's favorite tools, Janet thought. She could barely make out wooden wedges that were set on the floor of the platform at regular intervals so that Reynaldo's limbs wouldn't lie flat and would break more easily. The man with an iron rod in his hand began with the lower part of his legs then, slowly, ignoring Reynaldo's screams, worked his way up his body. As the man walked out of the chamber where he had tortured Reynaldo, he eyed Janet. Janet shivered at the way he had left Reynaldo. He would come back later to finish the job, or so Janet believed, to die slowly on the wheel.

"Janet, you are aware that Father Del Pierro and Reynaldo are evil, aren't you?"

"While I was under Father Del Pierro's care in the orphanage in Gilroy, California, he hurt me. I was young. I thought he loved me, but as I aged I was aware that what he did to me was rape and no one there would help me. They were afraid of him. Luci arrived and I was jealous of her and the attention favored upon her by Father Del Pierro. He stopped bringing me into his room. He replaced me with Sarah. I hated Sarah and I hated Luci. Father Del Pierro told me that they were unique in another way. I was the one he loved. When I turned eighteen, he sent me to the Philippines.

"I knew Reynaldo in this new country as my neighbors' gardener. I never knew that he and Del Pierro were lovers until Reynaldo betrayed me in my own home. Nothing Del Pierro does would surprise me. I did become suspicious when I didn't hear from Reynaldo but learned, like you, that he was in the hotel with Max and Luci. I didn't send him there so it had to be Father Del Pierro. Until then, I had no idea," she said with disgust.

"You don't like Del Pierro very much, do you?"

"Father Del Pierro got rid of me by sending me away to the Philippines. For that I am grateful, I received a degree and status."

"Is that it?" he asked.

"No, at my home he told me I was old and wanted to get rid of me. He hit me. Cardinal Saachio, tell me what you want me to do to Luci and Del Pierro and it will be done."

"Del Pierro doesn't trust you, Dr Gaetos. He feels you are after the treasure for yourself. Do you even know what the treasure is?"

"I thought it was from the lost treasure of Solomon. Am I wrong?"

"Only in part. Yes, there is a vast fortune hidden by the Knights Templar. I want that treasure, but I also want the diary that tells the anti-Christ. It might lead to a codex that will help me attain a higher power within the church if I can destroy it. I'm in charge of the Banco Ambrosio. They gave me this mission. Without the money and the codex, I will be ruined. The diary must be found and then burned."

"I will find it. I have an appointment with Luci at Chartres, and I think she is on track to find the key."

"I've been watching her. I think she is on to something as well. She's been separated from everyone she trusts. She's vulnerable. Get to her, take advantage of the situation, or you will end up like your friend."

Looking toward the door where Reynaldo was being held sent shivers up her spine. She was terrified. She could no longer hear screams, only whimpers, but she didn't care. Reynaldo wasn't loyal to her – something she didn't abide. "I'll get the treasure and the location the codex, Cardinal."

Cardinal Saachio looked at her and nodded. "Before the end of the week, the codex, written by Jesus, must be in my possession. We need to get the Italians back in charge of the church and remove the Gnostics who have become a plague in the Roman Church. The pope is in his last days and does nothing more than read the Old Testament."

"I will get it, Cardinal Saachio. I understand Max Dantie has been more than a little vexing in our pursuit of the codex. Luci has left him and called me to help her. I was on my way as her confidant to help her and guide her. Nevertheless, I think she is still enamored with Max and trusts him over me. We don't have much time after this."

"Tony is giving you men to help in your pursuit," he said. "Don't fail me, Dr Gaetos."

Saachio glared at Janet as she kissed his ring. Looking up, she caught Saachio's eyes. She had no idea that he knew about Antonio. They said that the eyes were the windows to the soul. If that were true, then Saachio had none. Walking toward the door, she no longer heard any sounds coming from the other room. She understood failure wasn't an option.

"Thank you, Your Eminence." Turning, Janet walked out the door.

Janet left with Saachio's bodyguard and headed out for the Chartres Cathedral in a limousine provided by the Roman Church. Their little group headed for the airport where a private plane was to take them directly to France. At the airport, loyalists of Saachio met them with guns to take out all who opposed Saachios' rightful place as head of the Roman Church.

† † †

In the next room, behind a door stood Sarah, listening to every word spoken by Janet. When Janet left with the bodyguards, only then did Sarah make her presence known.

"Ahh, my little dove. You have finally come home to roost. Come give your papa a hug."

Walking over to Saachio, her father, Sarah felt like a traitor to Luci. However, this was what she was meant to do. Her father was to become the next and greatest Italian pope in history. No one had the courage he did. Yes, he had sent her away after her mother had died in childbirth to be raised in a Catholic monastery run by Father Del Pierro. She was proud of her heritage, but she also loved and admired Luci and her family. It was sad that it had to come to this.

She had been Luci's sister and friend. She would always love her, but too much was at stake. Her father held the bank in the palm of his hand. Bertolucci, the manager of the Banco de Ambrosia worked for him, and soon, Saachio would have complete control of the Vatican and all the money. Saachio had helped his family back home by laundering money through the Banco Ambrosio. Saachio now owed money to the mafia and he could sell the codex and the treasure to pay off his debt. It would also elevate him to a higher station, after Bertolucci's untimely death, of course, and get the heat away from Saachio. Secret documents exposing the pope and his improprieties were to be leaked to the press. He would discredit the pope for his mishandling of funds from the bank.

"My dove, it is time for you to fly to France. Keep an eye on Janet. Do not trust her, and wait for Luci. If she discovers nothing, all is well. If she does, kill her and take the codex or we will be ruined."

"I understand, Father. I will be there as I have always been for Luci. However, Luci has been my sister. Her family took me in when I was in the orphanage with her. I owe her my life. She has protected me. Why must I kill her?"

"There is more at stake here than a few lives, no matter how important she is to you, Sarah. Now leave and help Luci uncover the missing codex."

The Roman Church was angry and went after anything that politically opposed its position. It was God's ambassador on earth. It gave the sacraments and it was to the church that the ordinary people gave their confessions so that God, through the Roman Church, might forgive them. The tarot was in the middle of this conflict. Pope Clements tried to stop the political dissent by banning the tarot, labeling it demonic.

To preserve their history, the Cathars created the tarot. After Jesus ascended to heaven, one of the three Marys secreted these picture cards to France – one of the cards was written by Mary Magdalene. It talked of angels who helped people transition to heaven. These scrolls were entrusted to the Cathars, in the hope that one day they would be located and brought out for the world to see.

The Tower

It is only with gratitude that life becomes rich.
~ Dietrich Bonhoeffer

Timothy continued to educate Luci about the cathedral with exciting information. Still, she thought about Max and wondered if she'd made a mistake not trusting him. "What did you say?"

"The crafters of the Chartres were not working on a clean site. They had to clean the rubble and surviving parts of the old church as they built the new. The south porch was where most of its sculpture was installed by 1210, and, by 1215 the north porch had been completed and the Western Rose Window installed. Each arm of the transept was originally meant to support two towers to flank the choir, and there was to have been a central lantern over the crossing – nine towers in all."

"Two towers?" Like the tarot card …

"Yes, plans for a crossing tower were abandoned in 1221, and the crossing was vaulted over."

As the guide was telling her this information, Luci began looking up the two towers in the book on tarot cards. "According to this book, many years ago, the towers were square or rectangular. These round columns were not common until the return of the Templars from the Middle East in 1127. Timothy, can I pay you to continue my tour after your lunch so I can see the North Portal?"

It was where she believed there was a clue from the twin tower tarot card and the possible location of the codex. A blazing red sun with scalloped rays is found in the upper right section of the tower card. One ray strikes the tower top from the stone battlement. Stones fall to the ground including a female figure in white. Could this point to Montsegur where Corba jumped? The other sun ray is striking where Loup and Esclarmonde rode with the surviving Cathars. "It would be a pleasure."

"Can we meet at one o'clock?" Luci asked.

"I will look forward to our continued adventure."

Luci walked into the museum gift shop and picked up a book on saints and another called *The Cathedral of the Black Madonna*, written by Markale. She thought she might find some information that would help her understand more about the location of the window that had the White Lady in it. At one, she left to meet with Timothy.

"The North Portal is right over there," Timothy said, pointing to the Holy Modeste, a carved figure called the White Lady.

Luci remembered from her childhood that the Lady had a happy, but secretive smile. "Some believe this statue is a tribute to Esclarmonde, who supposedly secreted out a treasure of great importance," Timothy said.

Luci looked closely at the White Lady and saw that she was holding a card in her left hand and, in the right, her fingers were pointing to the rose-colored windows, the one the guide in Scotland had spoken of. The Roman Church allowed no statue or tribute to Esclarmonde. But here in Chartres, a man who was secretly a Knight Templar had the statue erected in 1902. Here it remained, pointing the way, Luci thought.

Her phone rang. Looking down, she saw that it was Janet. She ignored the call since something caught her eye. Walking over to a window, she slowly and methodically looked over the etchings in search of some clue to guide her. Seeing nothing of substance, she looked away, but then remembered that in the window there was a sun. Just like the tarot Sun card, it was rising in what appeared to be morning, and cast a shadow over a circular walkway. *Could this be the pilgrimage that people take toward salvation?* Luci thanked the guide for his information.

"But we're not done. You've paid for two hours."

"That's okay; take the rest of the time for a break." Luci had an idea, but she would have to wait until just before the church museum closed its doors.

The Sun

Be kind, for everyone you meet is fighting a hard battle.
~ Philo of Alexandria

Striding out of the museum, she headed down the Rue de Seine to look for a second-hand shop. Spotting one, she bought a typical tourist outfit with thick, dark glasses and a camera to hang around her neck so she could blend in with the regular tourists who visited the Chartres museum.

Walking back to her hotel, she laid all her purchases on the bed, rang up room service and ordered French onion soup and wine. The concierge had told her how tasty it was.

"Thank you, ma'am. It will take approximately forty-five minutes to be delivered."

"That's fine, thank you," she said and hung up the phone.

Stepping into the hot shower, she thought about all that had happened since she left the university. Could it only have been a week? As she stepped out of the shower, she wrapped a towel around her body and looked at herself in the mirror. She had lost at least twenty pounds trying to stay two steps ahead of whoever was after Esclarmonde's secret. She saw cheekbones and her green eyes seemed a little lighter than they used to be. Hearing a knock at the door, she slipped on the robe that hotels usually provided, but before opening the door, looked out the peephole. She did not need any more surprises. She opened the door and the delivery boy wheeled in her soup, a loaf of French bread, and a glass of Chardonnay. She tipped the young man, shut and locked the door, then wheeled the food over to the desk. She used the hotel's notepad to write down the steps she needed to take for her plan to succeed. It was nearly three o'clock when she woke up. Feeling refreshed, she put the tourist clothes on and headed out.

She planned to get another guided tour and scope out hidden cameras and alarms. In her research as an archaeologist, she had traveled to many museums, and the curators had always taken pleasure in showing her their security systems, so she had an idea of how different museum systems worked.

Walking back to the church, she paid the general admission and slipped into the bathroom near the North Portal after her tour. She hid inside the bathroom next to the Rose Window, waiting for the church to close. One of the most interesting facts about the labyrinth at Chartres was that the famous Rose Window, set high in the east side of the cathedral, was hinged along the length of the nave, and would accurately overlay its pattern onto the labyrinth.

After guards checked out the museum, area by area, they locked up for the night. Luci thought about the history of the Chartres Cathedral. Could this be where they buried Esclarmonde?

The cathedral overlay the alignment and foundations of earlier Roman buildings. A druidic altar, the pavement labyrinth situated in the nave of the cathedral was riddled with confusion, supposition, and fantasy. Luci was determined to find the gravesite of Esclarmonde. The Tower card had pointed her here.

Although the nave of the cathedral was lined with chairs, and most of the labyrinth was subsequently obscured, it had long been a tradition to remove the chairs and uncover the labyrinth to allow people to walk it on Fridays. In the main nave Luci took out her pen flashlight and made her way to the Rose Window which was next to the White Lady.

Working her way along the nave, Luci heard a noise behind her. Panicked, she turned off her penlight and hid in a vestibule. In ancient Roman times, this was a partially enclosed area between the interior of the church and the street. Stopping to listen for which direction the noise was coming from, she quietly waited until she saw a woman with dark black hair tied back into a bun enter. It was Janet. She was making her way toward the North Portal. Shocked and confused, Luci did not make herself known. Instead, she decided to follow her. Luci knew now that Janet was after the treasure and she'd be damned if she helped the woman in any way.

Janet veered left toward a semicircular chamber located near the Lubrius Crypt. It was lower than the rest of the crypts. Janet walked straight for the shrine of a local saint.

So Janet thought that was where the treasure was located. Fuck her. Luci was pretty sure she knew that there was no treasure here, but possibly the remains of Esclarmonde. Turning cautiously, Luci backtracked and headed to the far end of the main altar next to statues of Green Men.

In 1123, a fire had damaged the town of Chartres. The North Tower was built immediately afterward by the remaining Knights Templar. They created two towers and it was intended that the towers flank a central porch. When the North Tower rose to the level of the second storey, the south addition began. Evidence lay in the profiles and the names of the masons marked on the towers. Luci put her penlight in her mouth and slid her hand down the wall where the names of the masons survived. Slowly, she looked for the name Guilhelm. If his name was here, she knew that Esclarmonde was close. One by one, she read the names silently until her fingers touched that one name, Guilhelm.

Esclarmonde was here.

His name was near the end and the last letter was written sideways, pointing her toward another way. Looking in that direction, Luci crossed back over toward a nave where the *Sedes sapientiae* – Throne of Wisdom – was located near the lower part of the Rose Window. The Throne of Wisdom depicted scenes from the Infancy of Christ that dated to 1223. The scene included the lives of the saints as well as the typological cycles and symbolic images of the zodiac and labors of the month.

Luci continued her journey toward the Western Rose Window, which depicted the Last Judgment. The center showed Christ as the Judge, surrounded by an inner ring of twelve paired roundels containing angels and elders, and the outer ring of twelve roundels showing the dead emerging from their tombs. Angels were blowing trumpets to summon the dead to Judgment.

Luci crossed to the North Transept Rose, dedicated to the glorification of the Black Madonna. In the center, was the incarnation of Jesus on the left and the Old Testament's prefigurations and prophecies on the right. The Virgin was holding Christ on her lap, just like the tarot card of the Empress, but she was pointing to a large statue of the White Lady.

As Luci reached out to touch the White Lady, a hand slammed over her mouth and someone pulled her against him.

"Keep your mouth shut, Luci," he said. "Del Pierro is here looking for Janet, and Janet is looking for you."

She nodded and Max slowly removed his hand from her mouth.

She knew the scent of the man who had grabbed her. "Del Pierro and Janet are back together?"

"What do you think?"

"They're the ones working for the church?"

"You're a pawn in a bigger game, Luci," he said. "I don't want you to be hurt, for God's sake, but you're screwing with the wrong people. You need to trust someone, don't you? So choose. Choose incorrectly and you are on your own. I can find the treasure without you."

"No, you can't. I hold the key," Luci had to trust someone, and Max was the only one who hadn't tried to kill her. *Yet ...*

"There's your pathetic ego again. You think your academic skills are going to show you the way?"

"No. I really do have the key," she said, taking her teddy bear and pulling out the key.

"I'll be damned," he said with a smile. "Okay, where to?"

"We need to make our way back to the labyrinth."

† † †

Janet entered the Rayonnant Cathedral, an arm of the church that the new artisans began working on in the thirteenth century. She searched out the new system called the terraced roofing. It was designed by more modern architects and consisted of overlapping stone slabs supported by stone beams resting on transverse arches. This resulted in a crawl space above the tribune vaults accessible from below by stone trap doors. She figured that under the recesses

156 L LEE KANE

of the vaults there was something hidden, a burial ground possibly.
Suddenly, she noticed Father Del Pierro looking at someone in the
wings of the church. Quietly, she reversed her direction. She was
finally going to put an end to all of this. Pulling out her gun, she
screwed a silencer in place.

Walking around the arches so she wouldn't be noticed, she
watched Del Pierro round the vestibule. He was almost in sight.
Raising her arm, she cocked the 9mm, squeezed the trigger, and
just missed hitting a Green Man carving.

† † †

Del Pierro heard the ping echo in the chamber and looked up just
in time to see Janet racing down the stairs toward him. Scurrying
away, he hid behind an alcove in the hope that she would come
this way.

† † †

Janet was determined to kill Del Pierro but she had to get to Luci.
Del Pierro could wait for a while longer.

Antonio was near. She just needed to call out and he would
finish Del Pierro off.

Del Pierro's attention was back on Luci and now Max. He would
keep an eye on things by staying hidden in the clerestory windows.

Esclarmonde's Diary

March, 1212
Loup pulled me away and put me on top of my horse. Together,
we rode out of Montsegur to the caves that surrounded France and
hid with fellow Cathars. Every night we would ride to resupply the
stronghold of Montesegur until the castle finally fell. I watched on
top of a hill as our citizens were chained together and thrown into
the pyres that the Roman knights had built. The red flames rose to
the heavens.

We rode close enough to watch the destruction, looting, and raping of our family and friends. Montsegur had fallen.

Loup knew what I was feeling. He also knew that I carried Guilhelm's child. So we had no choice. We had to safeguard the treasure and the child.

We took the treasure to a place where no one but the faithful would find it. We traveled by night to the caves of Auch where our brethren had hidden.

"This is a good place to die, Loup," I said.

"You know they are coming for us. The Seneschal of Toulouse is not far behind us. I have little hope and little fight left in me," I said.

Loup smiled at me and, together, we rode into caves.

When we entered the caves, we were greeted by many of the people of their homeland.

"We need to fortify the caves," Loup told the bishops.

"It is too late," one told him. "They have already surrounded us. It is a trap. They were waiting for you."

Loup took hold of my hand. He knew these caves better than anyone did. As a child, Loup had wandered this valley and camped out with friends. If anyone could get us out alive, it was my brother. On foot, he took me down a path, deeper and deeper into the cave, near an underground pond.

Loup was unfamiliar with this section of the caves. In this particular section, many a man had gone in and never come out.

"On my order, wall up all of the entrances to the caves," one of the knights said. "We will stay until we hear no more sounds coming out," the seneschal commanded.

Our fellow Cathars stayed near the front of the cave, giving us time to find a way out and a place to hide the treasure – Solomon's ring, and the Cathar codex.

Following Loup, I headed down a slope where we entered another cavern with water. Loup dove into the water and swam through the bottom toward a small opening.

The seneschal and his men stayed for over a month, listening for some sound to reach them from the granite interior. Loup would report to me on the activities of the guards.

Unbeknown to the knights, Loup had been watching them. Late one night when the guards had left the mountain believing we had all died, I swam through the small opening that led outside and rode to France to find a safe place to raise my child. Loup left for the Antioch Woods to continue to fight.

For their brethren, the Auch caves had become a tomb.

Strength

Religion is to do right. It is to love, it is to serve, it is to think, and it is to be humble.
~ Ralph Waldo Emerson

Luci aged 30
"What are we looking for, Luci?" Max asked, following her toward the labyrinth.

"Right around 1221, when the construction of the cathedral was essentially finished, the Masons moved on to finish the other parts of the labyrinth in the church."

"So, where are we going?"

"Chartres was designed according to proportions which obey the law of the Golden Mean."

"You mean the distance between pillars and the lengths of the nave, transepts, and the choir are all multiples of the Golden Mean?"

"Yes, and the ribs supporting the vaults of the quadrangular units of which the cathedral was composed is in the shape of the golden rectangle."

"I've been here so many times but never noticed that the overall ground plan design of Chartres is a Latin cross. It's quite a feat of human imagination and determination."

"Where we're heading is a brass or copper plaque that decorates the center of the labyrinth. It bears a representation of the combat between Theseus and the Minotaur. Under the plaque, I believe, lay the remains of Esclarmonde. That is where the White Lady from the Rose Window points. There should be a lock that this key will open there."

† † †

Because Max did not like enclosed spaces, to get his mind off of what they were about to do, he asked Luci about the history between Theseus and the Minotaur.

"It's quite a long Greek story. The Labyrinth, possibly the building complex at Knossos, was an elaborate structure designed and built by Daedalus for King Minos of Crete. Its function was to hold the Minotaur, a mythical creature that was half man and half bull that had been killed by the Athenian Theseus with the help of King Minos's daughter. Daedalus had so cunningly made the Labyrinth that he almost didn't escape it after he built it.

"Now here we stand in the middle of another labyrinth. I believe that the Minotaur is a warning to all who enter that, if they aren't careful, they'll never find their way out."

"What are you saying Luci?"

"Max your loyalties are with the Vatican. All I want is the truth for Esclarmonde, Corba, and the Cathars. Can I trust that, when I finally give you the key, you won't leave me locked up somewhere down in that labyrinth to die?"

"I've got your back. We'll find the answers we're both seeking and I won't harm you. Now, I guess that means we'll be going down into the burial grounds of Chartres together."

Turning away from her, he walked over to the copper plaque, then kneeled down to see if there was anything loose. The Minotaur on the plate is a warning for anyone who goes searching below, "Glad I brought my flashlight and twine. We can tie the cord around us so we don't become separated from one another. I think you're right."

"I can see you're not fond of underground chambers," Luci said. "Do you want me to go first?"

"No, just a little claustrophobic," he replied, suddenly remembering her panic attacks.

"I guess we all have our weaknesses, Max."

"Yeah, let's just go," he said

"Okay, Max," she said with a smile. "I do know that the most important feature of the Chartres labyrinth is the halo of ornamentation that surrounds the outer circuit of the labyrinth. It's comprised of the Wands, Cups, Swords, and Oracles of the tarot. It's called the *lunation* and refers to ancient symbolic meaning."

"Actually a man named Critchlow first coined the word luna-tion," he said. "When one divides 112 by four – the major divi-sions of the paths of the labyrinth – we find it gives us twenty-eight. The days of a lunar month? Some believe that the labyrinth served as a calendar. It offered a method of keeping track of the lunar cycles of twenty-eight days each. Using this method, the Roman Church could keep track of the date of the lunar feast of Easter."

"Is it a part of the tarot?"

"No. If anything, like the zodiac symbols that are in many artworks, it told the people when to plant their crops, water, and seasons. It had nothing to do with the tarot. Okay, here it is," Max said, kneeling over the plaque. "I see where you could use your key to turn the sphere. Do you want to do it?"

"Yes, I've waited a long time for this."

† † †

Watching the couple from the wings of the cathedral, was Janet.

Even in the academic world, Luci continued to outsmart her. Through deceit, Janet had moved up to become dean of the archeological department. Still, at every opportunity, Luci showed her up, making her appear a fool in front of her colleagues. Janet wanted her dead and she wanted the treasure. Screw Saachio. She was waiting for her opportunity to strike. She saw that Luci still held onto a teddy bear that Janet remembered from the orphanage. She was astounded when the woman pulled out a key and handed it to Max.

"It was within my reach all these years," she said to herself with anger and disgust.

† † †

Turning the key and using considerable force, Max was able to dislodge the plaque that had been in the same place for centuries. He opened it, and they peered down into the dark abyss.

Spotting a ladder made of rope, Max prepared to climb down. He turned around to make his way down when Janet flew at him and pushed him over the edge. Max fell down into the cavern, catching one of the rungs before crashing to the bottom.

Luci screamed and rushed to make a grab for Max. Janet turned quickly toward Luci and slapped her hard in the face. Luci stood where she was, shocked. Janet pulled a gun she had kept in her purse.

Luci gathered her senses and made a lunge for the gun when she discovered what Janet was doing. Using her skills as a martial artist, Luci broke Janet's wrist.

The gun fell to the labyrinth floor. "You should kill me, Luci. Because I swear I will be coming after you and I promise you that I will kill you."

"Give it up, Janet," Luci said, tying Janet up with the twine. Luci left to find Max, and see if he was okay.

"Oh, Luci, I've waited so many years to kill you. Reynaldo killed your parents. I blew up your home with the help of your house-keeper. But none of us were allowed to hurt you. You held the key, the knowledge that Del Pierro and Cardinal Saachio have been waiting for. And all along it was in your stupid bear."

"I've always known you hated me, but never why. You have to be insane to have waited this long to confront me."

"Insane, no; patient, yes. Watching you suffer has been worth the wait. You're so insecure, you've never known who to trust. No, Luci, I don't want to confront you. I want you dead. Do you understand that last part? You've always been a little dense," she said, laughing hysterically.

Out of the corner of her eye, Luci spotted someone coming out from behind the edge of the nave. It was Nick, he was still alive.

"Luci, I'll take care of Janet. You go find out how Max is doing."

"I thought you were dead, Uncle Nick. You fell from the library window at Yale. How did you get here?"

"I checked myself out of the hospital to come find you. I'll be fine, Luci. Now, go."

Without a second glance, Luci ran to the opening to see if Max was okay."

"Look, Nick," Janet pleaded. "We can make some kind of arrangement. The Cathars can keep the codex. All I want is the treasure."

††††

Nick slowly pulled out a ceramic knife. He'd carried it because it could be taken on a plane in his carry-on. He loved it because it was undetectable even by metal detectors. After his near-death experience at the hands of Del Pierro, he'd stayed in the hospital for a week, then checked himself out. He had a job to do to protect his niece, but, even so, he hated that he had to do what he was about to do.

Grabbing Janet with one swift motion, he stabbed her in the gut. He dragged Janet out of the labyrinth floor to the terraced vaulting where he had seen her earlier. Grasping her hair bun, he unraveled it like a veil then tossed her down the crypt where martyrs were buried. There Janet could die a prolonged and painful death among the people who had bravely fought for their beliefs only to die at the hand of the Roman Church. Hearing her plead for her life, Nick closed the lid of the crypt then hurriedly walked back to the labyrinth where he had left Luci.

Behind an alcove, Sarah watched all that was going on. She called the Vatican and told her dad where he could find Janet. Quickly, she hung up the phone.

† † †

Luci swiftly descended the rungs of the rope ladder to the ground. She prayed that Max would be alive. She felt arms wrap around her. It was Max.

"Oh my God. I love you, Max. I thought you were dead," she said, wrapping her arms around him and crying.

"I love you, too, Luci. We're going to be okay, let's get going."

Sarah raced toward the labyrinth just in time to see Father Del Pierro follow Max and Luci. Keeping herself at a safe distance, Sarah reached the opening, then slid down the ladder. Looking at the ground, she saw the footprints and cobwebs that had been disturbed.

The Hierophant

Differences of religion breeds more quarrels than difference of politics.
~ Wendell Phillips

Max began searching for his flashlight after he got Luci safely down and found another cavern lower than the one they were in. He began to descend another ladder, but it was difficult to see. Only shadows danced off the cavern walls from his flashlight. Abruptly, he hit bottom.

"Come down very slowly," he said. "This is a very old ladder and it's about a five-foot drop. I need you in one piece."

"Is it because of my winning personality?" she asked nervously. Her hands were wet with perspiration. She was tired and scared. Suddenly, her hand slipped away from the ladder but she quickly caught hold again.

"Be careful, Luci, this place is rickety." His eyes were adjusting to the dark of the underground burial site, his ears attuned to what might lie below them and what might be happening above them. He didn't know which made him more nervous.

Overhead, he could see the flutter of bat wings. A few insects made their way down his arm and he shivered. The gun he had brought was in a holster in the back of his jeans. It was reassuring to know that it was still there, because if there were bats and bugs, there had to be another way out but someone could be waiting for them. He didn't know what had transpired with Janet and Father Del Pierro and he didn't like surprises.

As Luci touched the ground, she let out a sigh of relief and wiped her brow of sweat. It wasn't from the exertion, but certainly from the anxiety of climbing down an old ladder into what could have been an abyss. She'd heard the noises up above and her acute hearing picked out the sounds of someone screaming. She knew it would be impossible to go back upstairs to find out what was happening.

Max used his flashlight and scanned right and left.

"Over there, Max. Those are coffins. During the Merovingian and early Carolingian eras, the main focus of devotion for pilgrims was a well-known crypt called the Puits des Saints-Forts, or the *Well of the Strong Saints*. It's believed that the Knights Templar buried the bodies of local early-Christian martyrs. There are names on the caskets. Can you read them?"

"Yes, this says, 'Here lies the body of Saint Piat, martyred under the cruel governor Rictius Varus, in the year 286 BC'."

"Well, what's he doing here?"

"Saint Piat according to my catechism class suffered a horrible death. His body was pierced with large nails that are used in joining rafters. They began his torture at Tournay, but he was finished at Seclin."

"Well, it would be a kind of identification, wouldn't it?" she asked nervously.

"Right. In the eighth century, the body of St Piat was taken to Chartres, and part of him still remains here in the Church of Canons."

"Look, Max! On top of his coffin is the zodiac sign of the Bull. It represents the Hierophant."

"I give up, what is that?"

"In the tarot, it's the sign of a holy man. It makes sense if you understand that the Hierophant's purpose is to bring the spiritual down to Earth. That's where the high priestess connects to the esoteric with her secret, possibly of the Cathars. The Hierophant strives to create harmony and peace in the midst of crisis. Saint Piat made every effort with his rituals, rites, and traditions to remind the community of their values, their shared identity, and the religious structure that gives their lives order and meaning. No matter how chaotic and frightening the times, he tried to bring tranquility to his community."

"Didn't bring him much peace, did it? He died a horrible death." Flashing his light to the left, Max spotted an ornate coffin with the lady from the Rose Window displayed on top.

Luci raced over to where the light shone and fell to her knees. "This is *it*, Max!" Gingerly brushing off the dust that had accumulated over the years, she read, "Esclarmonde, the White Lady.

Max, this is her coffin. Oh my God, we found her," she said with earnest, while gently touching her face to the coffin.

"Luci, we need to get out of here. I can hear something up above. What does it say on the coffin? Read it to me and then let's move."

"It talks about her life, how she died several months after giving birth to a son." Luci smiled, knowing that Esclarmonde had made it to Chartres.

"I wonder if the baby survived?"

"I'm not sure we will ever know. Maybe the Cathars got the baby to someone safe in France."

"What else does it say on the coffin?"

It wasn't so much what it said, but what she'd spotted. "I don't see anything else, Max," she lied. She had a seen a cylinder in Esclarmonde's left hand. Gingerly, she took it out and slipped it into her pocket. "It says nothing but her name on the casket." Luci decided to keep the secret of the cylinder to herself. But she needed Max to get her to Montsegur. "It states here that her brother Loup was buried with a box."

"Let's go," he said.

"There is more written around her, Max."

"Save it. We need to get to Montsegur."

Deciding to keep this information for much later, Luci followed Max as they made their way to where the bats were flying out of the cave. Tangled foliage blocked their way and the going was slow. Dried twigs and leaves crackled underfoot, and, once, Luci slipped on bat guano, but before she hit the ground, Max grabbed hold of her.

"You may say that you love me but you still don't trust me, do you, Luci?"

"Now why would you say that?" she asked.

"You keep trying to avoid me and you won't look at me."

"As you can see, I'm trying to stay upright. Thanks for the save."

Finally, they made it to a point close to where the cave opened to the daylight. Max shut off his flashlight and they walked out after pushing a lot of foliage away from the entrance. Surprised, they found themselves in the middle of Tivoli Park where they had taken a walk together.

†††

Sitting on a park bench, with a hat and newspaper hiding his face, Nick watched as the two left. He followed them to a car rental agency.

† † †

As they drove along the precarious pass toward Montsegur, Luci looked out at the scenery at the hills where the Cathars had made their last stand. At Montserrat, they parked their vehicle, and, like every other tourist, Luci marveled at the site before her. In her mind, she felt she could be standing where Esclarmonde and Loup made their escape on horseback while carrying the treasures.

"Luci, in this brochure I picked up at the café we were eating at, it states that many people have speculated that the treasure we are after is the Holy Grail. Montsegur was named as a candidate for the Holy Grail castle and there were linguistic similarities in the Grail romance written by Wolfram von Eschenbach's Parzival. In Parzival, the Grail castle is called Monsalvat, similar to Montsegur and meaning the same thing: safe mountain, secure mountain."

"That sounds very promising for you, but don't forget, Montserrat is supposed to have ties to the Holy Grail as well."

Ignoring her remark, he continued, "It's believed that the Holy Grail could have been one of two things: The Sangrail, which, in Old French, means royal blood. They believed that Mary Magdalene was pregnant with Jesus's baby and fled to France to carry on the Merovingian bloodlines. It also could mean, The Sangrail, which in Provençal French means cup or basin, like a vessel that carried Jesus's blood after he was crucified. What do you think?"

"Who knows? We can speculate forever. I'm following the clues in the tarot. That's what Esclarmonde wanted. The treasure may have already been discovered, Max. Did you ever think of that?"

Max said nothing, just glared at her. He needed to find Solomon's ring. According to legend, Solomon's ring had God's name engraved on it, and it was able to command demons to do his bidding.

The ruins of the castle were perched at a three-thousand-foot altitude in the south of France near the Pyrenees Mountains. It was located in the heart of France's Languedoc-Midi-Pyrenees region. Montsegur dominated a rock formation known as a pog.

"What's pog mean, Luci?" He knew, but she hadn't spoken to him in an hour and he thought this would get her to say something. It worked.

"It means peak, hill, or mountain. Montsegur was relatively self-sufficient with a great reservoir system of cisterns for water, a metal forge for weapons, and an ample supply of wood to fire it. Meat and dairy products were not in high demand by the strictly vegetarian Cathars and supplies continued to trickle in thanks to Esclarmonde and her husband. The pog, on which Montsegur is perched, is riddled with an astonishing network of hidden caves which are still being discovered and explored today."

Luci kept trying to think of ways to get away from Max. She needed to call Sarah to get the list of caves that she was sure Loup may have been buried in. "Montsegur is referred to as the Holy Grail castle, where the Holy Grail is supposed to be hidden. There was a text discovered in one of those small caves near the castle. What's fascinating is that the document is written in Chinese characters, but that's all anyone knows about the book. Maybe there are more, but no one has found them yet. It would be interesting to learn how those books came to be there."

"There are hundreds of caves. Maybe we'll find a clue regarding Loup. You can go look for the Holy Grail. Now keep driving," Max said.

Luci didn't know what to make of what Max had just said. Could he be trying to divert her attention away from the caves where Loup may be buried? Maybe he wanted to get rid of her. She gazed out the window as they drove along the Atlantic coast just south of Bordeaux.

"Hey, I'm starved," he said. "Let's stop at the restaurant up ahead. We haven't eaten since in hours."

Arriving at the restaurant, she sat on a bench and looked at the surroundings, which were beautiful this time of year. Rolling hills, green pastures, vines, and grapes that later would be made into wine. It was a beautiful day. They ate outside and savored the local cuisine of moules mariniere, a dish of mussels with garlic, double cream, and lots of wine. It was quite tasty, and, after a glass of local wine, Luci began to feel more relaxed. In her gut, she knew they were getting closer to the secret that had been taken out of Montsegur. She had kept the cylinder of Esclarmonde concealed from Max. She planned to leave him in Montsegur.

It had never been her intention to become rich by finding and selling the Holy Grail. What she wanted was what Esclarmonde had wanted: a document written by Mary Magdalene, an apostle of Jesus. Loup and Esclarmonde had risked their lives to save his last words for future generations. The codex was written in Aramaic. She felt sure the codex was written in Aramaic, but wasn't as yet positive. She had to get the cylinder to Uncle Nick. The treasure wasn't in Montsegur. It was in Lodat, in one of the tarot cards it has a scene similar to the city of Lodat, another important Cathar stronghold in the region. It had attained fame during the Cathar Resurgence in the early fourteenth century. The resurgence was organized by one of the last known Cathar prefects, Pierre Authie, who was later tortured to death in 1310.

† † †

"I've been thinking. I find it hard to believe that, while escaping from Montsegur, Esclarmonde and Loup would be carrying a large treasure. First, because they would have had to travel light and, two, because the Cathars believed that everything on this earth, like wealth, was evil, so they wouldn't care about a treasure," Max said.

"Good point."

"You're looking for something like a document or manuscript?"

"Possibly," she said. "I just don't think that after all these years, there will be anything left that archaeologists wouldn't have already discovered. I texted Sarah while you were in the restroom, and she said there are many caves around here. I think we should separate and spread out, widen the search at Montsegur. What do you think?"

"I think that's a good idea. If we don't find anything, we can head toward the caves and search there. That way, we can cover more territory and possibly discover what others have not."

"Sounds good."

"We have our phones, and we can check in with one another on a regular basis. Did your sister send you a map of the different caves?"

"Yes. I'll send it to you so we both have a copy. After we get done with Montsegur, we can divide up the caves."

"Great idea. Let's go."

Sword

A small body of determined spirits, fired by an unquenchable faith in their mission, can alter the course of history.

~ Mahandas Gandhi

Now alone, Max called Bishop Giovanni. "Luci and I are getting close to retrieving the codex written by Mary Magdalene. That's what Esclarmonde's diary is leading us to."

"The pope will be very happy to hear this."

Max was a regular mercenary recruit who'd served in line troops in various armies. At one time, he'd served in Italy and that was why the pope, himself, had chosen Max to help him keep the *Fabrica* – particularly Cardinal Saatchi – in check. Max knew the language and was well versed in the history of Italy. He'd gone to Monterey to study at the International Institute when he'd been called by the Vatican to help in the search for the last recorded document where Jesus spoke his final words to Mary.

Max had been a standout in his unit. He had never thought of a life outside the army until he'd met Luci. He wanted a life and a family with her, but he still had a duty to perform that had yet to be completed. He hoped after it was all over, he would be able to give the pope the codex. But he doubted that after recovering the document Luci would ever forgive him for his duplicity.

He had lied to her. But the treasure and the codex belonged to the church, not the Cathars.

The World

Blessed are they which are persecuted for righteousness' sake,
for theirs is the Kingdom of Heaven.
~ Jesus, Mathew 5:1

Max walked over to where a building site had once sheltered a community of Cathar women at the end of the twelfth century. He could still smell the fear between the walls, the waiting, the hoping that they would all be spared from torture or a horrible death by fire. Early in the thirteenth century, Ramon de Perelle, the co-seigneur and Chatelain, had been asked by a Cathar prefect Raymond de Mirepoix and Raymond Blasco to make Montsegur defensible. They'd been anticipating problems from the pope. From 1232, it became the headquarters of the Cathar community in the Languedoc and a refugee center for *faidits* – outlaws whom the Roman Church had stripped of their lands and goods, thought Max.

These *faidits* were like an earlier version of Robin Hood. They'd waged a guerrilla war against the Roman invaders in small bands, hitting the papists where it hurt. They took money that wouldn't go to the pope nor the king, but to the nobility of Occitan and the villagers.

After the failure of the uprising against the French invaders and the defeat of Henry II of England by Louis IX of France, the Council of Beziers decided to destroy the last stronghold of Catharism, thereby cutting off the head of the dragon. In 1233, the Inquisition was officially instituted, empowering Dominican and Franciscan friars to prosecute heresy and demanding, according to the terms of the Paris Treaty, local secular authorities assist and enforce the Inquisition's actions. The Inquisition had spread terror throughout the region.

Max wandered around the last building site. He called Luci, but received no answer. He left Montsegur, impressed with the people who had given up so much to protect their beliefs against men who would not accept any other view but their own. A terrible price had been paid. The world lost Jesus's most sacred words, even though they'd been given to the Cathars to protect. They'd been destroyed by the Romans. Max was going to try to get the codices all back to the church, including the cylinder that Luci possessed.

He remembered that Monsalvat Castle was the last stronghold of the Cathars after the first Crusade. He felt sure that Loup had taken the treasure there. History 101 at Harvard was coming back to him. He remembered that a Renaissance church, built next to a castle, contained a black wooden image of the Virgin – carved, according to tradition – by St Luke, was in the mountains of Monsalvat. Montserrat Cathedral sat on these mountains and was thought to have also been the site of the castle of the Holy Grail. He would leave Luci and travel there.

† † †

Luci had left Max wandering the caves of Montsegur. She'd needed time to think. Holding the Tower tarot card, she felt she knew where Esclarmonde was guiding her to go next.

Before leaving the place of the Holy Grail, she stooped down to tie her shoelaces by a large rock. Out of the corner of her eye, she spotted something in the dirt behind a crevasse. Lodged about six inches down was the tip of a white wing. She could barely see it. Her heart was fluttering. Was this a sign from Esclarmonde? She secretively dug up the object with her Swiss army knife.

Carefully, she pulled out what looked like a stone dove. Luci wrapped it in tissue and placed it carefully in a side pouch of her backpack. She left Montsegur in search of a place with WiFi access.

Fortitude

If you have two religions in your land, the two will cut each other's
throats; but if you have thirty religions, they dwell in peace.
~ Voltaire

"Sarah, thank God. I have been trying to get hold of you for the
last hour."

"Sorry, Luci. What can I do to help you?"

"Have you looked up all the caves that I asked you to so I could
give them to Max as a decoy?"

"Of course, and I saved the ones that you asked for that are most
likely to hold Loup's crypt. I am sending them directly to you."

"I don't know if I have told you how much I love you, Sarah.
You are certainly a life-saver." Luci envisioned Sarah at her computer, back straight, head held high, almost regally. She had
changed from a duckling to a beautiful swan over the years and
Luci had never felt closer to her than this minute.

"Ahh, you're just saying that because I'm so good with the
computer. Those after-school lessons really panned out for me,
didn't they?"

"Yes, they did." Luci smiled. "It's great hearing your voice. I'm
heading out for the caves in the Lasset Valley."

"Really? I think you might want to look at the cave of Chauvet-
Pont-D'Arc. It was discovered in 1994 and contains the world's
oldest known cave paintings, some dating back as far as thirty
thousand years ago. Many tunnels have not been excavated."

"How far is it?"

"It's about forty-six kilometers from you near the commune of
Niaux in Ariège in the south of France. It's pretty famous and
contains many prehistoric paintings. But it's also from the
Magdalenian period."

"I'll put it in my GPS and make my way out there now."

"The cave is large and the quality and condition of the artwork found on the walls have been preserved for centuries. There's evidence that suggests a landslide happened there, maybe even the one that killed the group that Esclarmonde and Loup escaped to from Montsegur. There are even remnants of clothing from the Teutonic Knights and Cathars from the twelfth century."

"Wow, it *could* be the last holdout of the Cathars Esclarmonde wrote about."

Leaving Lordat, Luci rented a new car and drove toward the Grotte de Niaux.

Dusk was fast approaching so Luci had to get to an inn for the night so she could start fresh in the morning. There was a lot to read about Niaux and if she were to find the right tunnel, she would need to do more research. Thousands of people had been through this cave, but none had gone as far back into it as she was willing to go.

She checked into Hôtel du Laca not far from the cave. Luci booked one of the cabins near a garden that overlooked a lake. The room was basic, but clean, and had a great bathroom. She hopped into the shower, then put on a pair of jeans and a T-shirt. Finding her way to the restaurant, she went to the terrace bar where she relaxed with a Pinot Grigio and a rural country meal that was very tasty.

As she was savoring her dinner, she felt someone standing over her. It was her Uncle Nick.

"You've had long journey, Luci. You found the cylinder Esclarmonde had hidden away?"

"No, I didn't."

"I went into the labyrinth after you and Max left and noticed that something had been removed from Esclarmonde's hand."

"It was nothing," she said, looking down at her plate of warm food that was fast becoming cold.

"You and I know differently. Guard it well, Luci. Your friend Sarah has been accommodating, but be careful who you trust."

"Like you?"

"I can only try to protect you. I have kept Janet away from you; Del Pierro, too, as well as Max, though it's been difficult considering the appeal you have for him. I have not the education, nor was I destined to be the discoverer of the codex by Mary Magdalene.

The Cathars chose you long ago, Luci. The sooner you accept your fate, the easier all of this will be for you. You have the knowledge; use it."

Luci picked the napkin off her lap, dropped it on the table, stood up, and left the restaurant without a word to her uncle. He never warned her, never stayed in contact. Now he was saying Sarah was not to be trusted.

So much death could've been avoided if he had been honest and stayed with her.

Returning to her room, she picked up a map and noticed she was only a mile and a half out of Foix, her family's home. Tomorrow, if she had time, she would visit the Foix castle where it had all begun.

The next morning, Luci was up by four a.m. She didn't want another encounter with her uncle, so she left the hotel hungry, hoping she would find a café along the way. She drove past a gas station, but didn't see a place to eat, so she drove until she saw the caves directly ahead of her.

Parking her car, she saw a sign that offered guided tours through the caves. She waited for the next trip to begin. Hopping aboard the tram, she felt the struggle of the tram as it chugged slowly up the steep and narrow access road. It would have been difficult for a group of women and children with their heavy clothes and belongings to climb up here for safety. Walking through the entrance of the cave, Luci felt as if she was walking into a cathedral. Listening carefully while the guide spoke, she waited for her moment to break away from the tour because, in the caves, the guides went through the cave by torchlight to protect the paintings on the walls. Her moment came when the group turned a corner so Luci went the opposite direction.

She held up her phone as a flashlight and wandered back to an observation deck. Before she came to it, on the right was a ramp, and, just after, a locked gate. That was her destination, but walking through the cave, she felt as if she was back in the time of the Albigensian War. There was a wealth of exciting artwork and text written in Occitan, explaining the history and art of the cave. Luci was impressed with the detail of art and the superb sculptures. On the platform she could see the valley below. Coming to a gate that barred anyone from entering, Luci took out her Swiss army knife, she pulled out a long pick and jimmied the lock until it opened. Luci walked farther back to a hidden cave known as "Soulja d' Alliant," about one hundred feet before the Grotte de la Vache, which was the last refuge of the Cathars.

Long ago, it would have had a rope ladder or light wooden ladder that could be pulled up if they were under attack.

"I think we'll need this to see what's in the cave above."

Startled, she whipped around. "Shit, Max. What are you doing here?"

"Probably saving your ass again. You'd probably try and climb up there, fall, and break your neck. I brought a rope ladder. We can make it down that way."

"Thanks Max, I thought you'd still be in Montsegur." Following Max's flashlight, she exclaimed, "Oh my God. Look at these paintings. These are depictions of the tarot cards. Like the artwork, it's made of manganese dioxide for black, various iron oxides for red and orange, and the organic binders are possibly bird egg yolks or whites, possibly blood, or other organic materials, such as animal fats, that have stuck the pigments to the wall since the 1200s. The writings are pointing the way to where Loup must be buried."

"Look over there, Luci. I see something behind the rock."

"I think it is an underground chamber. Let me take a minute to look at the writing."

"Could you use a flashlight? Will that work?"

"I have my phone light, but yes, a flashlight would be better. Just point it at the writings, Max"

Typical of most cave art, there were no complete human figures, although there was one partial "Venus," a pregnant figure composed of a vulva attached to an incomplete pair of legs. Above the Venus and in contact with it was a bison head – the composite drawing many believed was of a Minotaur, very similar to the picture in Chartres Cathedral.

I wonder if this is just a coincidence. There are a few panels of red ochre hand prints and hand stencils made by spitting pigment over a person's hand and pressing them against the cave surface. Abstract markings, lines, and dots are found throughout the cave.

She took out her sketchbook and traced the lines and dots above the head of the Venus. *This looks like a map.* Quickly, she sketched out the rest of the diagram, then headed back out to the platform for a better look.

Remembering the amethyst on the cylinder she had taken from Esclarmonde, she saw it contained a secret chamber and a symbol of two intertwined circles centered on a line that ran through the amethyst. She also remembered that Max had a ring very similar to this same design.

Lifting the map she had drawn to the sun for a better look, she recognized that the same hand drew the shape of the amethyst on the cylinder and the map. Now she needed Sarah's directions to get the coordinates to locate Loup's burial cave.

"Luci, where did you get that cylinder?"

"In the crypt at Chartres Cathedral," she said defensively and turned her back to him.

Using the map she had found in the cylinder, she followed it toward another underground cavern with Max's help. "Look. It's the same symbol on the stone that's on the cave wall."

Luci struggled with the amethyst and pressed the stone to the rock, but she wasn't strong enough for anything to happen.

Max put his hands on hers. They heard a creaking sound, and, suddenly, the secret entrance of Loup's burial chamber began to slide open.

Max and Luci entered the chamber. There, in the corner of the cave, was a monument. On it, a single name was written. *Loup*. They approached slowly and Max looked for the Grail.

† † †

Max was obsessed with turning over the burial chamber to see inside. He continued to look around the chamber for a cup, like the Holy Grail or something that would be easy to carry while escaping from Montsegur.

Luci read the engraving on Loup's monument, then used the amythest once again to open a secret compartment where she found another tarot card.

The Joker.

The Chalice

Just a tender sense of my own inner process that holds something of my
connection with the divine.
~ Shelly

"Oh my God. There's a scroll from Thomas, James, and Abraham, and others in the coffin," Luci said. "It begins with Abraham. He knew Pontius Pilot would continue looking for Jesus's followers. It continues with the story of Judas when he was found hanging in a field and buried there ... paid for with the thirty pieces of silver."

Max wasn't listening to Luci, his eyes were on the box in Loup's hands.

Luci continued, "Joseph of Arimathea, a secret follower of Jesus's and Mary Magdalene's uncle, took the three Marys to Glastonbury, Scotland for a new life. He then left for Ariège with the documents. The monks believed that Joseph brought two silver cruets that preserved the blood and sweat of Christ and were buried with him near Glastonbury. His epitaph was written by Mary Magdalene, though it was erased later by people of the Roman faith. It said, 'Open shall these things be and declared to living men.' It tells us to search for the truth in Montsegur."

Hidden from Max and Luci, next to the minotaur, was Del Pierro waiting for Luci to discover the treasures. "Give me that document," Del Pierro said, coming up behind her. He pointed a gun at Max and grabbed the documents from Luci.

"Shit," she said.

"Put the gun down, Father," Max said.

"Don't give me that hero act, Max Trulio. Yes, I know who you really are."

"Since you know who I am, then you know you'd better put the gun down and get the hell out of here."

"Max, what's going on?"

"Hey, I remember you. I saw you at Yale."

"Let it go, Luci," Del Pierro said, moving closer to Max.

"I warned you. Stay where you are or I'll kill you."

"We're both on the same team, Max. We work for the same people."

"Except I don't want the documents destroyed. You do."

Del Pierro had a piece of paper in his hand. "Max, let me show you the letter from Saachio." Walking closer to Max, Del Pierro lit the paper he was holding and threw it, flaming, at Max.

Max's shirt caught fire. Just before he dropped to the ground, he shot Del Pierro, then rolled to put the flames out and saved the document.

Luci ran to help, but saw Sarah enter in the doorway.

Puzzled, Luci asked, "What are you doing here?"

"Luci, we have to get out of here. The place is old and filled with documents that are acting like kindling. It's too late to save any of them."

"My God, Sarah, these documents will be destroyed and a race of people who have long been forgotten will be erased from history."

"So could we."

"Max, oh my God, Max. Sarah help me. He's passed out and his pant leg is now on fire."

Luci and Sarah took off their jackets and started beating the fire off Max's legs.

"Luci, the smoke is going to kill us and we'll be trapped with the burning embers."

"We can't leave him," she said, looking at Max on the ground. "Help me drag him to safety."

"Luci, you need to hand over the box."

Luci stared at Sarah. "Why?"

"They belong in the Vatican, not with the Cathars."

"What are you talking about? You know Esclarmonde sent our family to find these documents and the treasure so we could expose the truth about the Roman faith."

"Your family, Luci, not mine."

"What do you mean, we're not family? I've loved you as my sister."

Sarah pulled out a gun and pointed it at her. "We can both get out of here, Luci. Leave Max and give me the documents. You don't have to die with him."

Sadly, Luci handed the documents and the box over to Sarah, but couldn't believe someone she'd loved so dearly could have betrayed her all these years.

"Leave, Sarah. I don't want to see your face ever again."

Sarah started to head out of the cavern, but she turned and said, "I do love you, my darling sister. But there is a higher purpose and you just won't listen to me."

Luci picked up her backpack that contained the cylinder and began dragging Max out of the cave. It was a long way and she wasn't sure she was going to make it. Then adrenaline started to pour into her body and she knew she wouldn't give up. One thing was for sure: she had given Sarah the wrong codex, not the one from Mary Magdelene. That was what Esclarmonde had wanted and that was what Luci had saved. The treasure box was irrelevant to Luci.

Max began to revive, and, holding onto Luci's shoulders, hopped with her out of Loup's burial chamber where Loup had laid for hundreds of years. In the distance, they could hear Del Pierro groaning. He was still alive. The cave was filling with smoke. She couldn't go back and help him, too, so she left him to die. She couldn't understand people. Why was one religious belief so important that people had to die? It never stopped. This wasn't what Jesus taught or what any prayer book that had been passed down required. She was sad for Del Pierro and Janet. It shouldn't have to be like this.

Max was getting heavier. Luci was straining to make their way out of the cavern. Finally, they were out, and a tourist came over to help her with Max. Escorted out by the cavern guards, they mixed with other tourist groups. A paramedic with a strange insignia on his shoulder came running over with a gurney and put Max on it.

"I'll take him from here," he said.

"Thank you," Luci said.

Max looked up at her with a smoke-streaked face. "I love you, Luci, but you've built that wall so high that no one can get in and you can't get out. I know it's so hard for you to trust me, but, on this one thing, please believe me."

"Ma'am, you should get yourself checked out for smoke inhalation," the paramedic said.

The paramedic took Max to an ambulance, then raced to the hospital. The ambulance wasn't the same color as the other French ambulances that were helping the tourists, she noticed. Luci ran back to her rental car to follow the vehicle that had taken Max. Ignoring the police, she tried to dodge the traffic but was blocked by the fire engines coming in to save Grotte de Niaux. Up ahead, she watched the ambulance slam on its brakes.

Max threw open the door and jumped out, racing toward Sarah.

Luci watched as it played out in slow motion. She saw Sarah climbing the hilltop where the Cathars had made their last stand. Sarah handed the codex and Loup's box to a man in a black leather jacket with a priest's collar.

Luci watched as Max ran up the hill after Sarah and the other man until they were all out of sight.

† † †

Luci drove back to Hôtel du Vache from the night before, then passed out on the bed. She turned the phone off so no one could contact her. She was exhausted and had many things on her mind that she needed time to work out.

The next evening after she woke up, she showered and changed her clothes, then went out to the restaurant. She needed time alone and ordered food to be brought to her on the porch that overlooked the lake.

Nick came over to her, reached out, and put his arms around her shoulders. "Where are the documents and the box that you had?"

"Sarah handed them to a man in a leather coat. Do you know something about this?"

"The Cathars believe that Saachio will give them to the 'Ndrangheta who he has been funneling money to through the Vatican. Solomon's seal will be given to them to repay money he has been siphoning off. I doubt if we will ever know for sure what will happen to them. By giving Saachio the ring, Sarah stopped Saachio from having the pope killed. That was his and the mafia's ultimate goal to kill the pope and take over the Banco de Ambrosio. He would then be able to pay off the debts and control the money from the Vatican."

"Unless Max stops them," Luci said.

Cups

History is philosophy teaching by example and also by warning.
~ Lord Byron

Luci aged 30
Luci left for Foix Castle in Montsegur where a Cathar church still survived. As she climbed Mount Pog, she turned around and looked below. The magnificent view of the village of Montsegur and the surrounding countryside was breathtaking. Just when it seemed she couldn't take another step, Montsegur's magnificent chateau appeared between the tree limbs almost like magic. She could envision Esclarmonde and Loup playing among the colorful trees.

Luci stepped inside. The aura of the ruins was positively intense. She walked into a small church that most castles had within them and saw a drawing of Esclarmonde on a glass window.

She walked around the chateau's perimeter and viewed the nearby mountain peaks. A man came toward her with a friendly smile. She felt that she knew him.

"Luci, I have heard about you from Nick. You look so much like your mother, my dear."

Smiling, Luci handed the amethyst cylinder over to the prefect of the Cathar Church. Without a word, she left Esclarmonde sadly behind.

At the Hôtel de Vache, Luci retrieved her backpack and the copy of the contents of the cylinder she'd had made at the hotel's business center and slipped it into her bag.

Pulling it out, she read the last words that Jesus spoke to Mary when he'd exited the cave the Romans had buried him in.

"Do not be afraid of dying, Mary. I died and was carried away by my guardian angel. The Creator knows us personally, hears us laughing, and watches over us when we are awake or when we sleep. When we cry, He is there with his arms around us. He sees us in our saddest moments, and He begs us to come home. I will send you signs so that you know you are never alone. Heaven is beautiful. We go into darkness. Everything is transparent, but distorted and blurry.

"Mary, I was conscious out of my memory. I saw Mark below me and my mother praying beneath the cross I had been nailed to. There was a rhythmic sound, distant yet strong. I could hear it from the place up above and it gave me hope. Each sound cut right through me like a heartbeat.

"I had nobody. I was there, in a place of pounding, pulsing darkness, but our Father was present. Everything was gone, as if transformed back to the beginning of time. Something happened in that darkness. I saw lights of white and gold and, as it brightened, the darkness that surrounded me fell away. I had left Purgatory and now was in a new place, closer to our Father. I heard a sound, a living sound, like the most beautiful piece of music I had ever heard. It grew in volume as a pure white light descended and obliterated the pounding that seemingly had gone on for eons.

"The light got closer and closer, spinning around me and generating those filaments of pure white.

"At the center of the light, something else appeared.

"The colors that surrounded me transfixed me into a world of wonderment. The colors were astounding. The hills were the greenest of greens. The water of the lakes was a beautiful deep blue. In the distance I heard something similar to a cacophony of sounds that, when combined, lightened my beating heart. The moment I understood this I moved up. There was a flash and I was in a new world, the most beautiful, glorious, colorful world I have ever seen.

"Brilliant, vibrant. I felt like I was now a newborn babe.

"Below, there was the greenest valley and I was flying, passing over trees, and fields, streams, waterfalls, and there were people of every race and color. Horses cantered about, dogs, cats, and every conceivable animal were all around.

"As I touched the ground, I realized I wasn't alone. A gentle-looking woman with long silvery blonde hair and green eyes took my hand without a word. Was this my guardian angel? We walked together on a patterned surface. It was alive with vivid hues of blue, green, silver, and gold, like the wings of a butterfly. The vibration of the wings was enchanting and mesmerizing.

"I could hear her speak to me though no words were exchanged. She told me that I'm loved and cherished by the Creator forever. There is nothing I could do that He would not forgive.

"I was with angels. I could see perfection, and I was a part of it. I was a part of all things in this world.

"I saw the abundance of life throughout time.

"Mary," Jesus said, "tell the people of the world that they are loved by the Father. Angels will guide them through the muddy lower levels of existence, through Purgatory to a higher plain to be one with our Father. We are all a part of the same Creator."

These were the words that the Cathars lived by and wanted all people to know. He will always be there for us, Luci thought. The codex was a treasure for all people. It was the last words spoken by Jesus. A message that he wanted to be conveyed to all people of all beliefs. That He loves us all, united under His love and protection.

The Fool

Historical sense and poetic sense should not, in the end, be contradictory, for if piety is the little myth we make, history is the big myth we live, and in our living, constantly remake.
~ Robert Penn Warren

Luci pulled out the last card in the tarot – the Fool or 0 – that she had found in Loup's crypt. She knew that she had come full circle. She had left the safety of her home in Monterey and gone in search of the last words spoken to Mary by Jesus that had been kept safe by Esclarmonde and the Cathars. Through Esclarmonde, Luci had become a part of the Albigensian crusade and the fall of Montsegur. She'd followed Esclarmonde's instructions, beginning with the Magician, through the events of locating Loup and the treasure they both took out of Montsegur before its fall. She met her long ago relatives – the counts of Toulouse, Corba, the heretic monks, and Cathar prefects through the eyes of Esclarmonde.

The Fool's number was symbolic of the circle; it represented wholeness. The Fool had now become Loup, the Cathar prefect in disguise. Loup fulfilled his spiritual quest, arrived at the top of his order, and sent his sister out to spread the word, so that, one day, the truth would come out about Heaven. Esclarmone achieved an understanding of the spiritual messages of cards: the Star, the Moon, the Sun, Judgment, and the World. She walked with her eyes uplifted to God, her clothes in tatters, running for her life so that others could find peace in death.

"You do not need a church for the salvation of your soul," Jesus said, "but merely strive to become a good person and cause no harm.

"Denounce greed and pride, and relinquish your worldly burden, including your attachment to your Self. Keep your gaze directed toward God and practise the teachings of love and compassion, even in the face of oppression. This is the true Church of God, the Church of Love. It is the path to salvation."

This is what Saachio, Del Pierro, and Janet had not learned and what they would never learn.

Luci left the church and headed for the airport to go home with a new perspective on life. At the airport, she picked up a newspaper to see if there was anything in the press regarding Chartres and the codices.

Madmen

A small body of determined spirits fired by an unquenchable faith in their mission can alter the course of history.
~ Mohandas Gandhi

The prefect of the Cathars had invited the news media, and all churches, temples, and mosques to be a witness to the last words of Jesus to Mary. The French newspaper covered it exclusively and it went viral. People boarding the plane Luci was flying home on were telling each other about the codices. It was hope for the future. No mention of wars was on the front page, nor the numbers massacred, nor the children who were murdered in schools, but, instead, hope for all humanity.

On the back page of the newspaper there was an article written about Cardinal Saachio, "God's Banker." A native of Milan, Saachio was an overseer for the pope of the Banco Ambrosiano, which collapsed in one of Italy's most significant political scandals. A source of enduring controversy, his death in London was ruled a murder after two coroner inquests and an independent investigation led by Max Dantie of the Swiss Guard of the Vatican.

Luci guessed Max prevented the sale of Solomon's ring, but what happened to Sarah? She wondered sadly.

Luci continued to read about Saachio's death in connection to the Banco Ambrosiano. The principal shareholder, the 'Ndrangheta, had used the bank for money laundering, prostitution, and the sale and distribution of drugs. The article went on to read that several billion euro had been exported illegally, leading to criminal investigations.

Luci closed the newspaper and slipped it into her purse. Sitting down, she waited for her flight to be announced. She had lost a colleague, Janet, although she had fundamental differences with the woman who believed money was more important than getting the truth out to the people of the world.

"Latte?"

Luci looked up and saw Max holding her favorite beverage. The one person she had been afraid to trust was the one who was always there for her. When their flight was announced, Max grabbed their bags and they walked down the aisle to their seats and to a new life together.

"Where is Solomon's ring, Max?"

"In a vault, deep inside the Vatican. Where it can never again be used against mankind."

Writer's Note: Fact or Fiction

There are some facts and much fiction in this novel. I described Heaven, it is what I want to believe, not what everyone thinks it to be.

Let's start from the beginning:

The Hanged Man: People were tortured unmercifully by the Roman Church by many methods. Did this really happen to Guilhelm de Montanhagol? It's possible since he was a Knight Templar and he did love Esclarmonde, who *was* a Prefect in the Cathar religion, though not the High Priestess.

The Wheel of Fortune: Was there a diary by Esclarmonde that was kept hidden by the Cathars? No, but there was something taken out of Montsegur by two riders two days before the Teutonic Knights raided, chaining every man, woman, and child together and setting them on fire. What was it that the two riders took out? Montsegur was the stronghold of the Cathars; many speculate it was the Ark of the Covenant, some, the Holy Grail. I have a hard time believing that possible, but an important document or small treasure could be quickly sealed, hidden, and taken out of the town.

Is the Cathar religion being practised today? Yes.

Esclarmonde's Diary: Was Loup and Esclarmonde's father Raimond Roger? Did he rape their mother, the Abbess of the Roman Church? Yes. I wonder why. Was the Count de Foix making a statement against the church? Did the Abbess die in childbirth? Yes. Was Loup sent away to a monastery, and was Esclarmonde taken in by Corba, her aunt? Yes.

Did Aunt Corba teach Esclarmonde about the Cathar religion? Yes.

Force: Do bad things happen to little boys and girls by priests. Sadly, yes. This has been accepted as standard practice over hundreds of years. The hierarchy of the church found it convenient to look the other way, even today.

Esclarmonde's Diary: Was Folques originally a troubadour who came from a very wealthy family? Yes. He entertained the lords and ladies in Occitan, the birthplace of love, chivalry, and poetry. Did Folques become a priest because Esclarmonde spurned his passion? This is purely conjecture. It is more likely that he could earn more money more easily than by being a troubadour. Did Esclarmonde meet Guilhelm at a party in her uncle's castle? Probably not. A Knight Templar, sworn to celibacy and God, would probably not attend this kind of function, especially when the Cathars in Occitan were under the scrutiny of the Roman Church.

Esclarmonde's Diary: Simon de Montfort was a soldier for the Roman Church, and would gain a lot of land if he defeated Raymond Rogers and the surrounding countryside. He stormed the castle at Beziers and murdered thousands. Did he know Esclarmonde? It's possible. Did Guilhelm ride to Esclarmonde's rescue? Purely my imagination.

The history from Esclarmonde's diary is, for the most part, an accurate account of the Albigensian Wars seen through the eyes of a Cathar. Having a journal was a way for me to pull the readers into a long-forgotten people in history who've been hunted, persecuted, and murdered because Pope Innocent III deemed them heretics.

In the thirteenth century, did Bishop Alaric tell his knights to kill everyone who sought safety in the Roman Church? Yes. He said, "Kill them all. God will know his own. Now light the arrow."

Many people of differing cultures and religions lived in that town and died that day.

The Moon: Is the history of the tarot cards exact? As far as I have been able to find out, yes. They were like baseball trading cards. The wealthy had artists paint their stories on lambskin which they then passed about. Could the Cathars use this to memorialize their religion for centuries to come? It's quite possible, and having the traveling gypsies hand the cards out to families of Cathars would be an excellent way to spread information of the time.

Were there two factions in the Catholic Church? I believe there were and quite possibly still are. Did the Banco de Ambrosia bring together the Vatican and the Mafia? Well, where there are power and money, there usually is corruption. So it is highly likely. Does the *administratia* of the Catholic Church want an Italian pope in the seat of power? Quite possibly.

Esclarmonde's Diary, June: Corba was the prefect, not Esclarmonde. Corba's son died at Aimer de Montreal at the battle of Lavaur. Her daughter was captured by Roman knights and thrown down a well to her death.

Is there a Cathar woman depicted in a stained glass window at the Cathedral de Chartres? Yes there is, but I don't know if she is a Cathar. Many of the Knights Templar switched allegiance after reading a sacred document that Esclarmonde took out of the library. In France, many of the Cathedrals are named after Mary. Which Mary? Is it Mary, mother of Jesus or Mary Magdalene or Magdali, from upper Nigeria, known as the Black Madonna? I'm not sure. The Knights Templar did become the Freemasons and built many of the cathedrals. Did Joseph of Arimathea and three Marys leave for France? That does seem to be true. It's also been said that Peter pushed the boat out into the sea, rudderless. Why? Was he jealous of Jesus's love of the two Marys? And who was the third Mary? I have purchased several tarot cards and have used the definitions of the cards to keep the messages true to that period. The tarot cards date back way before the 1100s and only became a form of fortune telling recently. Maybe it was a diversion by the gypsies to throw off the Roman Church.

Everything I wrote about the Rosslyn Chapel is true. And many say its benefactor took many important documents to Canada for safekeeping.

Madmen and Strangers: Many of the things written about the 'Ndrangheta are true. The names were changed to fit my story and the history of this branch of the Mafia was taken from newspaper articles and the Internet.

The lullaby and ballad I included in the story were not my creation. They were from the Occitan people's heritage. I felt the reader should know how vital the troubadours were. The songs, the lullabies, and their culture were vibrant in many ways.

My interpretation of Heaven comes from my Catholic upbringing, books I've read as a teenager, and a movie that starred Robin Williams with the brilliant colors. When I was in my teens, I read a book about a woman who'd died and what she saw in Heaven.

They all gave me inspiration and the direction I wanted to impart to you, the reader.

The death of Pope John Paul and the threats against Pope Benedict so that he would resign, have been written about, and speculated upon for years. I don't believe we will ever know for sure if they are true or not. The Vatican is sealed off from the masses and is a power beholden only to itself.

I hope you have enjoyed the history of the Cathars and look forward to the continuing adventures of Luci de Foix.

www.ingramcontent.com/pod-product-compliance
Lightning Source LLC
Chambersburg PA
CBHW050403030726
47503CB00006B/1997